RAZOR COUNTRY

NICHOLAS WAGNER

Copyright © 2024 Nicholas Wagner

All rights reserved.

ISBN: 9798874216689

PART I

Sun-soaked specks bled through the tavern window and flitted about Colm Steiner's knuckles as he rhythmically knocked the splintered table bearing his burned down cigarette. He was wiry, with dark hair trimmed neatly, blue eyes and light stubble on his chin. He wore the ragged remnants of a hazel herringbone three-piece suit, with an M1911 holstered beneath, and black, mud-speckled boots. The newspaper in his other hand was from Sydney. Two weeks old, it recounted the murder in the desert territory where he now found himself.

In recent years, he had been involved in undermining nascent labor movements in Guyana and the Bahamas. His employer in those matters informed him by telegram of events in Australia requiring his attention. One of the upstart cattle operations attempting to grab a foothold there was run by the son of a British magnate, who, having encountered some trouble in the UK, evidently sought to terrorize the southern hemisphere.

According to the newspaper the son was, besides a failed cattleman, apparently now a murderer as well. Bertel Wight, described as a fit, amiable, blonde-haired man in his late 20s, was the primary suspect in the slaying of a fellow rancher, Jenrick Thoresby, allegedly over a border dispute.

Having perused the story a third time, Colm thumbed through the remainder of the paper while awaiting his guide, a Dharoug named Dolon Parsley. He entered the tavern wearing a white shirt, tan pants and brown riding boots. He sat down across from Colm and began sipping coffee from a chipped cup.

"Two days, then."

"On horseback, yes," Dolon replied. "Rough country all the way."

The men said their farewells to the portly barkeep reading his stained magazine and walked through the doorway into an ocean of pale light.

They mounted horses and set off into the uneven brush dotting the dry basin of the plateau, which dissolved into a hazy endlessness ahead. Colm possessed not even an animal's raw instinct about the place, his mind lingering on disputes settled thousands of miles away. The tracker ahead, along with the sun scathing the air, seemed to him a recurrent reprisal, himself a bit player presaging the end of certain things in certain places. Harbinger of unwelcome changes. Colm wondered if any of the ancient gods remained hidden in the stones nearby, made refugees in their own land by the curious whims of foreigners.

When night fell, they burned a campfire and ate a kangaroo Dolon had shot the previous day. The dark blanket of sky hummed above with a warmth calmed by evening. Colm swiped insects from his neck and watched Dolon twist grass into wheeled designs as he fell asleep.

The next morning, they made coffee over the fire before they once more resumed the slow rhythm of the parade along the plain, each step of the horse scattering the muted, muggy rage of the atmosphere. Their journey was a hostile negotiation, their steadiness a prayer against complete annihilation.

Colm sipped water from his canteen and considered conversations from the other side of the world. An attempt at bribery that ended with a murder along a riverbank. Far off, the mirage of nothing re-articulated into shapes. Brush cut into a pen, cows within. Beyond that, two wooden shacks behind the dark wood of the house.

Colm slipped from his saddle without charm and gave the reins to Dolon, wiping his face in a futile attempt to rid himself of the environment, but it had seeped into him. When he knocked on the door and encountered the woman, he was as much a delegate of the desert as whatever civilized measures he was hoping to impose on it.

She had stringy blonde hair, face ripened deep with exposure, wore a filthy white shirt over black pants. She looked at Colm with unflinching humorlessness, smoking a cigarette like a burden from a lost bet. There was a revolver in her right hand.

"Gaffney, is it?" Colm asked. "Gaffney Wight?"

"Sure," she said.

"Colm Steiner. I'm with your husband's people. Back in England."

"Too late for that."

"Regardless, there are things I must do here."

"So as not to impinge on the business prospects of the relations."

"And if your beloved slips the noose as a consequence, would you shed a tear?"

"Not a happy one."

"As I suspected. We'll be imposing on your hospitality now."

"You know what a barn looks like. Have at it."

She walked back into the house. Colm and Dolon found the musty, dilapidated structure out back, walking past thirty or so scraggly cows that had congregated to stare at the visitors. There were vacant stalls within where the men tied up their animals, then found the nearby well and filled buckets for their troughs with water and then oats.

As the sun ached red and gold in the distance, the men went back to the main house, and the three shared beef stew in the bleak, cramped wooden kitchen while Colm attempted to get a better handle on things.

"What's the situation here. From your end," said Colm. "You'll want to be honest, especially if there's some unpleasantness that needs to occur. The paper says someone was grazing on someone else's land."

"If by land you mean twat."

"I'm guessing by the tone you're the aggrieved party. The man's wife?"

"Daughter."

"Right. And there were complications?"

"No, no, all went as planned, regarding nature's designs for the process."

"Conception, then. Is this child still among the living?"

"Only because I haven't finished my supper," she said, lingering nefariously on the last word.

"I'd advise against your direct action in the matter."

"I'd advise you keep your fucking mouth shut at my table."

"I'm here to soften the blow of recent events. But I could just as easily land another one. With paper. A body might recover from a knife or a gunshot, but the laws of man obliterate. It is his legacy, perfected. A law is violence manifest. It is entirely bereft of action, it destroys at suggestion. Does that inspire awe within you?"

Colm lit a cigarette and studied the woman's face, his eyelids widening and narrowing as he drunk in her features.

"We take these things for granted. Society, I mean, not you personally. But I feel as though you must as well. I look at you, and I feel shame. For you. The human species, really."

"You can't say these things to people," she said.

"They send you places. The men," Colm gestured upward. "The men upstairs. And they give directives regarding comportment. Regarding alacrity. Ways to effect their designs. And you find yourself maneuvering through a landscape they're not even interested in understanding. Which is a very long way of saying, you'll need to be more forthcoming, Miss Wight. Because a fire follows us, and we're pouring gasoline."

She motioned for a cigarette from Colm's breast pocket, and he lit one for her.

"You'll handle this to my satisfaction," she finally asked.

Colm nodded. She grabbed a scrap of newspaper and drew a map.

"Half day at most," she said.

"How many are there?"

"The mother, Bernice. Her slattern, Meredith. Two men I usually see there, on and off. They've got others."

"And you?"

"Three-day hires from town."

"Resuming duties in the morning?"

"Day after."

"Where's he gone to?"

"Not the fucking foggiest. Doesn't know anybody in this godforsaken country. The ones he does would shoot him on sight. Out of principle, maybe. They came here to get away from his lot back in England. Think that's half of it with the floozy. Did it 'cause he could. Only apparently he couldn't. Who fucking knew." She stubbed out the cigarette.

"You are, unfortunately, as it regards my moral leanings, on the winning side of this particular conflict..."

"You are a fucking prick. Let's not keep doing this, go find my husband."

"You shall be reunited with your mangy cocksucker in due course. We'll be taking the barn, I presume."

"I don't give a fuck what any bit of paper says, I'll toss this lead through your lungs if I see you again before morning."

"Very well."

Colm and Dolon exited the house and made their evening preparations in the barn.

When morning came, they followed the poorly rendered map to the next ranch in much the same country as they had traversed, a shimmer speckled with dark plant life, flatness sluicing into vague promises of a horizon. Knuckles of rock revealing themselves from betrayed promises of civilization. Finally, they saw the two cows that had escaped from the ranch cavorting in the center of the worn-down dirt that constituted an emerging road.

Dolon and Colm encircled them, and without much prodding, the fugitive creatures returned to the ranch nearby.

It was not unlike Bertel's property, the build of the house done by a steadier hand. Two aboriginals were about, and one walked over to lead the cows into a pen on the back side of the house. The other walked up to the visitors, his hands hooked in the suspenders over his ratty t-shirt as he looked up at them from beneath the withered hat brim.

"We need to speak with the Thoresbys," said Colm.

The aboriginal forced a smile, seemingly aware of some guile afoot, but led the men to the house anyway. The other keep his head down and busied himself in a shack on the opposite side of the pen.

The aboriginal went inside the house and returned with the woman. Dark hair tied back, gentle eyes, a simple black dress. She possessed a demeanor too soft for the country she now inhabited. When the pleasing register of her voice appeared with her first words, Colm was not surprised, and in his mind, it prefigured some tragedy.

"This is about my husband?" she asked, smiling through a true grief.

"It's quite hot out here."

She led the men into the house.

Inside a kitchen nearly identical to Gaffney's, Bernice

served the men tea. Colm heard the rumblings of her daughter in the next room.

"We're looking for Bertel Wight," Colm said.

"As are others," she said, defensively.

"Not as hard as we are."

"What are you asking?"

"I'd like to ease your suffering. The suffering of those involved in this misfortune."

"Murder. Can you call it that? Do they allow you such ethical considerations?"

"Inasmuch as they don't hinder my obligations. We can talk about allaying the grief done here in a more practical sense once I've located his persons. Once we've dispatched of exigencies, legal or otherwise..."

"I am to aid you in a maliciousness against my own persons? Against my daughter? These are egregious demands."

"I don't often make promises, given the mercurial nature of the world. I wouldn't wish to be branded a liar. But I promise you, there are ways this can get worse. And they all begin with you not telling me the things I need to hear. How do I find this dreadful man?"

"He was friendly with my husband. And apparently..."

Bernice gestured into the back room, where her daughter slept.

"Then I will speak to her. In your presence."

Bernice walked into the back room, woke Meredith and brought her into the kitchen. She was in spirit but not form, her mother's twin. Blonde instead of brown hair, heart-shaped face with large ears, in a white night dress. Pregnant with both a child and a look of scorn.

"They're searching for him too," her mother said.

"Will you murder him?" asked the girl.

"No," said Colm.

"Then why should I tell you anything?"

"All that's good in the world is bought with unpleasant things. Such as what you're feeling now. Interest paid against the misery of tomorrow. Until all debts are settled at the end."

"You'll make it okay?"

"I will try to," said Colm.

"He would talk about us going away. He had seen a mission on a river. He said there was peace there. We would sit atop the rocks, and he would point to it."

"You'll show this to me?"

The girl nodded.

They all walked outside, an evening redness painted the desert. The aboriginals were still nearby, smoking in chairs beside the pen where they'd led the cattle back in for the night. With her fingers, the girl traced a path in the desert. Then the women went back inside the house.

Colm and Dolon mounted their horses, found a spot a short distance away to set up camp, made their evening meal, and slept. In the morning, they followed the girl's phantom hand until the land slunk lower, and cooled, and emerald sprinkled with angled trees pocketed the slopes along the water winking the sky back at itself.

The horses drank, the men filled their canteens, and they marched through the thicket until the settlement rose in wooden slants. Two rows of plain, thatched houses, at their terminal, a chapel only slightly larger than the other buildings. A few aboriginal children were foot racing in a flattened lot between the mission and the wilderness. There were women cooking, men smoking.

Organ music flowed from the church, the two men followed it.

Beyond the rows of pews, past the pulpit, was a piano in the back left. There, a gray-haired European woman in a white dress played "My Life Flows on in Endless Song," while a group of aboriginal children sang along. When the number was finished, the children dispersed, and Colm walked over to her. She had a bob of curly hair, blueish-white on closer inspection, and an uncertain grin.

"Good afternoon, my name's Colm Steiner."

"My name's Edna Doyle, I run the mission here with my husband, Felix. What's this about, then?"

"I'm looking for a man named Bertel Wight."

"Regarding what?"

"Things you don't talk about in churches."

From behind Colm's shoulder, the door opened, and Felix entered. A balding man with a handlebar mustache, in a white dress shirt and black pants. Still a commanding presence in his old age, he walked over to his wife.

"What's going on here?"

"Just politely inquiring about a man's whereabouts."

"Well, you'll talk to me about that. Go on, Edna."

Felix shooed his wife out of the chapel, placed his hands on his hips and with his small mouth puckered in a serious pose, wordlessly demanded an explanation.

"I just need to know where he is."

"You're not the law, what is this?"

"I'm with his people."

"Then he'll find you when he's good and ready."

"It won't work that way, I'm afraid."

"I suspect we've reached an impasse here."

"I appreciate your time," Colm said, and walked out of the chapel.

Colm and Dolon walked their horses away from the mission, a small crowd of aboriginals having gathered to witness their departure.

"I'd wager the minister there's helping. We'll just follow him next time they leave with supplies," said Colm.

"And if not?"

"Whatever's down that road."

"Probably not any answers that way," said Dolon.

"And yet, there's where we'll find ourselves."

Before they'd gotten out of the village, they heard the woman's yell. They turned to see the source. One of the natives in a yellow dress had run from the furthest thatched dwelling, and began hollering, over and over again:

"Mary!"

Felix and Edna and a few other locals swarmed the girl, her face a stream of tears, and took her back into her house. Colm left the horses with Dolon and walked over to the house. When Felix finally emerged, his flustered face erupted.

"What'd I tell you earlier?"

"Listen, this man, Bertel, is on something of a spree. Just tell me, has he taken the girl with him? Mary?"

"Could be one of the boys here did it."

"You have some regular mischief makers lurking about?"

Felix crossed his arms, kicked at the dirt.

"Suppose ol' Bert's worth looking into," Felix finally relented. "Together, maybe."

Felix gathered three men from the village, and on horseback, the party traveled along the bottomlands to three houses constructed in the same manner as the village, all overgrown with thick foliage.

"Site of the old mission," Felix said. "Raided, chapel burned down. Figured to move upstream. Better luck there."

Felix dismounted, walked over to the nearest building, and knocked on it. "Hey, it's your old pal."

There was scuffling within. Finally, the door creaked open, and Jenrick appeared in the crevice, face drenched in sweat, eyes wild as if with illness. A beard distinguished him from his newspaper photograph.

"What's going on in there, mate?"

"Less interesting than what's going on out there. What are all the men for?"

"Girl's gone missing."

"I could help look. I'll meet you fellows back at the new mission. Or just let me know which way you're going."

"How 'bout you step out for me?"

"I need to clean up, it's unseemly, is what it is..."

Felix forced the door open, and as he did, Bertel's revolver blasted him to the ground.

One of the mission aboriginals fired at the shack, and his companion pushed his rifle down.

"You might kill the girl!"

The shuttered window facing the men opened at once. The revolver rang out again and shot one of the aboriginals through the throat and he fell off his horse. Bertel howled in agony as he regained his senses, writhing in the soil, his stomach a motley of gore.

Colm and Dolon rode into the trees, out of the revolver's range. One of the aboriginals went to stifle his partner's bleeding, and as he did Bertel emerged and shot him through the skull and he dropped. The remaining aboriginal returned fire, the blow winging Bertel.

"Fuck," he yelled within.

The last aboriginal rode for cover behind another tree, then trained his rifle on the window.

"What do you suggest?" Dolon asked Colm.

"We want him alive, they don't."

The aboriginal and Bertel exchanged fire, each missing. Felix twisted in the dirt, continuing to howl in agony.

Colm motioned the remaining aboriginal over, and he trotted to their position.

"Ride back to the village and get the doctor, we'll keep him here."

The aboriginal stared at the carnage and reluctantly agreed, retreating down the road.

"Bertel," Colm called out. "My name's Steiner. I'm with your people. Your father's people, back in England."

"So fucking what?"

"So we could ride out of here right now."

"Yeah?"

"Yeah, it's your lucky fucking day. Where's the girl?"

"Which part of her?"

"They'll be back from the village with more guns, do you wanna be here when they arrive or fucking some whore in Sydney?"

Bertel emerged from the shack, revolver drawn, his white shirt stained with new and dried blood.

"Fucking Steiner. I've heard of you, yeah? Some dead men in Guyana."

"Let's just say I'm not welcome back."

"I fucking bet not."

"Get your things, let's go."

Colm walked over to Felix, skin now pale from the profuse blood loss. He reached his hand weakly up at Colm. Colm looked into the house, saw Bertel packing a small satchel with clothing. Beside him, a bloodstained sheet covered the girl's body, only her feet were visible.

Bertel emerged.

"Let's fuck some whores, eh mate?"

As Bertel walked over to the dead aboriginal's horse, Colm drew his pistol and shot him through the back. Bertel briefly twitched in the dirt, then died.

Colm walked over to Felix and held the wound in his stomach until the other aboriginals returned. They took Felix back to the village first, then returned for the dead men.

The two new widows and Mary's mother wailed in the streets for their people as they arrived, bodies wrapped in sheets atop the horses. Edna wept at her husband's bedside until he awoke the next morning.

Colm and Dolon left before the chaos settled, with Bertel's body strung up on a horse behind them. Riding past Bernice and Meredith's farm, he beckoned the women outside, and they gazed upon the three horses in the road, glazed in sunset. No words exchanged, the men again embarked on the road to Gaffney.

"Shot in the confusion," Colm explained the next morning, in Gaffney's front yard as her workers led the corpse-bearing horse into the barn.

"That right?"

"It is."

"How will the news strike your employers?"

"Not well, I'd wager. But I've explained away worse. The father seemed ready to be rid of the mess. You blame the women still?"

"Not hearing the rest of it."

"Good."

Dolon watched astride his horse along the road. Colm finished speaking with the widow, and mounted his own.

"We part here," Dolon said. "Too much blood."

Colm nodded, paid him what was owed from a small satchel. They shook hands, then Colm headed back along the road towards Sydney to contact his employers. Dolon took the road in the opposite direction, where there were no answers, but he was going anyway.

PART II

Colm found a phone in a roadside hotel, and dialed his superiors in London. Given the body count, they seemed pleased with the outcome. They gave him wire instructions for the remainder of his pay, and told him to remain nearby for a case developing in the area.

He drank gin and slept with angry prostitutes. His people finally contacted him later on in the week about a missing brothel owner from Surry Hills named Priscilla 'Prisca' Posher, who slashed up her husband and fled south with their savings. The prostitution charges never stuck, but they'd gotten her bereaved spouse to flip, so the attempted murder was their best chance at permanently shutting down her remaining establishments up north.

Police had lost track of her until they received an anonymous telegram at the beginning of the month placing her in the company of Winifred Napoli, aka Wynnie the Knife, who'd run sly grogs in neighboring tenements in Sydney until she'd been chased out a few years previous. They'd met in an asylum for wayward teenagers, and briefly worked together in a brothel in Darlinghurst. Current intelligence placed Napoli in a town called Perpetua, a half day's ride from Colm's whereabouts.

It ran ahead of the frontier on account of a silver mine that dried out after three years, but the cattle rush that came shortly after kept it afloat as a way station.

As Colm left the hotel the next morning, the hookers grimaced at him from their rooms above, tossing drinks and cigarette ends, professing their undying affection with a volley of curses. He rode along a dust-strewn road of modest vegetation slightly more civilized than the ones he'd known the previous weeks. He passed a preacher and his wife driving a stagecoach of belongings east. A Model T spooked his horse about noon.

The two-story hotel loomed above Perpetua's two rows of modest wooden stores lining the road. To its far right, down an incline, was the abandoned silver mine that disappeared as one neared the town, save for the ramshackle of tracks, administrative buildings and workers' living quarters that were partially collapsed down the dried cliff face.

Colm went to the hotel, then stabled his horse in the livery around its rear, feeding and watering her. She'd been with him several weeks now, and he'd yet to name her. He'd thought it overly sentimental to call her Mary but found himself doing it anyway.

The building next door had a newly thatched roof that slunk down at a severe angle towards the street, as if hastily repaired in the recent past. There were patches in the walls where the boards had been replaced, darker than the rest. No sign indicating it was anything other than a residence, but jazz music hummed low from a phonograph when a woman stepped out into the street.

She had a crimped blonde bob, a dark shade of sad wide eyes, and wore a loose black dress tied with a red velvet sash. The bare left calf above her flats bore a burn mark like a checkerboard. She stumbled as she struck a match against the bottom of her shoe and lit a cigarette dangling from her mouth.

"Have you ever witnessed such distilled elegance?" she

asked Colm once she noticed him staring at her.

"I thought I'd stumbled across an opera until you opened your mouth."

"And now you're sure of it."

"The wild inventions of our age. Telephones. Automobiles..."

"Graceless women and awkward conversations," she offered.

"No, you're a mint. Caught your shine from the road without seeing it."

Colm tapped himself on the temple with an unlit cigarette, which he replenished in flame.

"What's in here?"

"Bad things, darling."

"Bad things like you?"

"Worse even. Women. Booze. Cards."

"That arm's far too lovely to lack some complement within."

"I make no promises one way or the other, I simply vanish like some fairy tale destroyer, luring helpless travelers to their doom."

She stepped backwards into the establishment, and tossed her half-finished cigarette into the road, waving him into the sly grog with spooky movements of her hand.

The room was a smoke stream interrupted by dull curves of orange and blue lantern light from the walls. The left half of the room was empty wooden tables. There were two women within, the one behind the wooden counter of the bar area to the right, surrounded by bottles and barrels, had slicked back dark hair and sleepy blue eyes. Her black, sleeveless dress clung to her frame, cut off about mid-thigh.

Another woman, gray-haired and much older than the other two, had fallen asleep on a couch in front of the central staircase beneath a newspaper. Seated beside her was a foppish man with slicked down, golden hair, a fine mustache, his suit a dandy shade of bright yellow.

From a glass jar, he daintily chewed pistachio nuts one at a time, swiping his fingers prissily against a bright blue handkerchief on the couch's arm.

"Oh my," he said in an exaggerated drawl. "What have the kind spirits of this country brought into our establishment?"

He stood and walked over to Colm, inspecting him with a bizarre energy that made Colm reach for his pistol.

"Unnecessary. Ask me why."

A shotgun shell chambered upstairs. Colm saw the serious, diminutive man in the dark suit and bowler hat aiming it at his chest from the landing.

"Don't worry about washing up tonight. Ribbon's got your new outfit down his barrel, bright red with a hint of buckshot. There are beautiful women here, friend. Can't have any firearms turning their faces into some kind of mashed up mess. Make it awful hard to sell the cunny attached to it."

The fop took Colm's gun.

"This is a serious piece of machinery."

The fop walked over to the couch and sat down. He unseated the Colt's magazine, then ejected the last round.

"My name's Lausanne."

"Drescher," said Colm.

"Have you entered our establishment with a pure heart and purity of intent?"

"I've done my best to hollow out my worst instincts."

"What more can be asked of a man?"

Lausanne returned the dismantled weapon to Colm.

"Let's leave it in pieces this side of the door, shall we?"

Colm nodded, walked over to the bar and ordered two gins. He downed the first, then held the second as the blonde woman from outside walked back over to him.

"Drescher, then?" she asked.

"That's it."

"Call me Checkers. Bit of a joke I guess, on account on the love mark down there," she said, gesturing to her wounded leg.

"That was love?" he asked. "What does a man like that make the other thing look like? Hate, I mean."

"The inside of a pine box. What parts they find."

She looked upstairs at Ribbon, who waved at them. Colm waved back.

"How long have you hung your hat here?" he asked her.

"It's gathering dust," she said.

"Where else?"

"All over."

"Sydney?"

"Not so much. We had a farm south of here. Spent some time in Melbourne."

Colm thought this narrowed the search down at least, she seemed to be telling the truth.

"How about you?" he asked the woman tending bar. "You like Melbourne?"

The dark-haired woman shook her head. In contrast to Checkers' giddiness, this silent barkeep possessed a haunted quality.

"What's her name?" Colm whispered to Checkers.

"Celia."

Prisca. Priscilla. Celia. Fits, thought Colm.

Two gentlemen in suits entered the room, one a lanky fellow with a thin mustache. He took Checkers by the arm.

"I just have the hour," he told her. "Let's go."

They were up the stairs before Checkers' drink had time to finish spinning on the countertop. The other man, large and bald, sat down at a table near Lausanne, and they started talking like old friends.

Colm turned to Prisca.

"I was in Sydney not too long ago," he said.

"You'd like some type of medal for making it out?"

"I just meant, there's more places like this there. I'm finding the sporting life in this part of the country a little underwhelming."

"You could fuck a kangaroo," she said.

"I have fathered so many bastard children among the animal kingdom, they've barred me from entering zoos."

Prisca snorted a little, concealed her amusement with a rag.

"One more, yeah?"

Colm tapped the table, she filled his glass with gin.

"Will you be here tomorrow?"

"I might be," she said. "It's not a definite thing, I'm not regular, like...if you want something regular, there's other girls."

He stared into her face, smeared thick with eyeshadow and rouge, quite pretty. There was a misery strung across her bones beneath the pleasing features.

"I'm no good right now, but I'd like to see you tomorrow."

"That'd be okay. Like I said, I'm not a regular."

Colm paid for the drink then walked next door to check into the hotel.

He used their telephone to call the office in London, and had the secretary, a prickly old woman named Clotilde, see if she could find any more details on Prisca to make sure he'd got the right person. Clotilde dug through her files with grumpy sincerity and in her gravelly voice said:

"Identifying marks include a tattoo of a white duck above her right hip."

"You're an angel, Clotilde."

"Truly. And you are sent from hell to test me. Be gone, demon." She hung up the phone.

Colm slept peacefully in the small wooden hotel room, and wandered the town before his next encounter with the target. As he walked to the general store, he caught his first glimpse of the legend, Wynnie the Knife, dumping a piss pot from the window in the house beside it. She exited, in dark glory, curly hair a fantastic mess, darting eyes gathering the scene about her. Her black dress seemed designed for some hellish wedding, maybe.

She walked into the general store. Colm lit a cigarette and followed behind her. He leaned against the sill of the door, and watched the owner, a thick redheaded man in a brown vest, hand her a cut of the till. She admonished him, then walked outside.

She gave Colm a once over and stopped in the street to address him.

"State your nefarious purposes in this town."

"I conjure spirits," Colm said, dragging the smoke.

"And I cast them away," Wynnie said, flicking the cigarette out of his mouth before stomping it to death in the dirt.

"You have bewitched my heart," said Colm.

"And you my bowels," she replied, walking off.

Colm bought some razors and tinned food from the general store, then attended to his horse. He smoked away a portion of the afternoon reading the newspaper on the veranda, watching the little trials of the town play out below him.

A brown-haired girl and her brother kicked a ball about the street. A preacher left one of the houses and walked into another, but Colm couldn't figure out where they held the ceremonies without a chapel. Visiting, maybe. He saw a man in filthy rags dig around the waste of the mine and fall asleep beneath a cart.

When evening descended, he washed himself in a basin and trimmed his beard. He ate his canned meat, drank coffee and walked into the grog again. There was another girl there this evening, with thick blonde hair to the puffy shoulders of her blue dress. Her face was caked up in a garish theatrical style, heavy white and rouge.

The mustached man from the previous day sat beside her at one of the tables, whispering into her ear, while she stared disinterestedly at the ceiling and drank herself numb. Wynnie was behind the counter, Prisca nowhere to be seen.

"Were you not dispersed into bats and brimstone?"

Wynnie asked Colm.

"By some unholy ritual, I was revived in the blood of a virgin. A shameful thing all around."

"Shame to waste a virgin, rarer than silver 'round here," she said.

"Where's Celia?"

"Gin was it, yesterday?"

Colm nodded. She passed him his drink.

"And the other spirit. The one for my soul."

"She's beside herself. Unwell."

"Is that right?"

"What could make it wrong?"

"A number high enough," he said.

"You think me a monster. Willing to risk the well-being of a dear friend for a few coins." Wynnie leaned across the counter. "And you'd be quite right. Tattle!"

The girl in the chair roused to attention.

"Let the tramp upstairs know she'll be having company." Wynnie turned to Colm. "Finish your drink. Buy another for yourself and your lady."

Colm passed her a handful of coins and motioned for the bottle. He walked it upstairs.

Prisca sat atop a red velvet cover, in a light blue night dress.

"I know you're not feeling well. I just wanted a word. Needed one really, after being struck by your beauty yesterday."

"You're a lying bastard. And so is Wynnie. I'm not sick," she said. "I slept through the liquor delivery this morning and she didn't want me to have any cut of the johns tonight as her spiteful recompense. She drive up the price some?"

"I'm sure she did."

"Spew out the rest of your romantic nonsense before we get down to it, then."

"It's quite embarrassing actually."

"Better here than church."

"I have an abrasion along my abdomen," Colm said. "I was told it was a birth mark."

"You'd like me to inspect it?" she asked.

"You're having fun with me, but I'm quite serious. I was told all those who have committed egregious sins are preordained to do so by such a mark. Would you consider yourself a sinner?"

"I'm all rot and vinegar," she said. "If you're half-serious at all, and I think not, I'd say some folks were pulling your leg."

"All the same," he said.

"Very well, I may have missed it myself," she said, rolling her dress up to reveal her stomach, and the small white duck above her right hip.

"I can't tell from this distance," he said.

"Closer, if you must."

He leaned in near her stomach.

"By mouth, perhaps," she said.

He kissed her stomach.

When it was finished, they lied heaving beside one another, utterly undone. She pulled her dress down, walked over to the window, and stared out at the desolate vacancy beyond the mine.

"Can see miles ahead through that nothing, and I'd swear there's a hundred creatures I've missed clawing their way towards me. It's a vicious thing, this patch of earth at night."

"Why you?"

"Because I know enough to fear them. Wouldn't that be half of it? Some beastly presence, getting its kicks in first."

"I can hardly fathom the habits of men," Colm said. "I'd hate to misjudge the dead as well."

"Fair enough. Let their ravenous consumption of your entrails remain morally ambiguous."

"The hero of one side..."

"Is the flesh-eating ghoul of the other. That old

chestnut."

"Would you see someone outside of this place?"

"Has the half step from your hotel become an unbearable voyage?"

"There be monsters along that road. Snakes. Quicksand. Traveling salesman."

"Should the occasion arise, I could see myself meeting you elsewhere. It'd have to be quite grand though," she crossed her arms. "Like an execution, maybe. Better still if it's yours. I haven't seen a man I've slept with hanged, though I've often imagined it."

Colm began to dress himself.

"Very well, I shall begin masterminding some bungled crime that I might become better fodder for your amusement."

She bared her neck for a parting kiss, but he proved too ravenous, and she ended up pushing him out of the door.

As he lay in bed smoking that evening, his mind wheeled away at snares that might enclose Celia once she'd lost the protective cocoon of the grog. He'd have to isolate her at some distance, and perhaps dispose of the two guards, though it'd need to be outside of the building.

There was no answer to his woes the next morning, and he thought to give her some breathing room lest he scare her off entirely. He trotted Mary along the outskirts of the mine, where a few drifters idled around the former workers' quarters.

He gave an elderly gentleman with long silver locks a cigarette and asked about scenic landmarks nearby. The man gestured into the desert. Colm followed the path to where the shimmer settled into rock mounds forming a wall. Ahead of it, a screen of desert oaks threw shadows back onto the wall.

Colm purchased a few novels from the general store and waited out the day.

He thought to broach the topic with her that evening,

but happenstance brought the magician into town early that afternoon. Colm watched him check in from the banister on the upstairs landing of his hotel. He had short gray hair with a matching beard and a black suit. He gave the innkeeper a perfectly winning smile as he carried his two suitcases up the stairs to the room next door to Colm's.

"Good evening there," he said, placing his suitcases within the door's threshold before stepping back outside to speak with Colm. "I must tell you, though I adore this country of ours, its lesser animal life has made a trial of the romance." The man demonstrated a snake bite on his lower right arm.

"Thankfully I had my kit ready." He extended his hand for a shake. "My name is Howell Pritchett."

Colm shook the hand. "Colm Steiner."

"Are you a permanent fixture around here, Mr. Steiner?"

"I couldn't say so."

"Are you staying long enough to take in some entertainment?"

"Above board or salacious?"

"Slightly less than wholesome, accounting for accusations of witchery."

"You are a magician."

"Was it my vague allusion to the occult, or has my face finally grown into the part?"

"You have a slightly chilling aspect to your appearance, Mr. Pritchett. I didn't want to comment for fear of giving offense."

"None taken, for when one dabbles in the void, it often returns with the spectator. Regard none of this lightly."

"I shan't. When will I have the pleasure of seeing your show?"

"The glimpse beyond the veil of all things known will occur first tonight in the charming business next door, with repeated performances tomorrow and the day after."

"Then I count my blessings, Mr. Pritchett. And I wait with bated breath."

An hour before the sun set, Colm went next door to see Celia, who was again working the counter, while two farmers chatted with Tattle.

"You'll have a great view."

"I've seen him already in Sydney. Worth checking if he's improved."

"You're really selling him to me."

"They put a picture-house in overnight?"

"You're right, I will watch, and I will enjoy."

A few drinks later, the magician appeared, as did Wynnie, Tattle, the guards, the preacher and the mustached man from the previous two nights.

Pritchett produced his suitcase and laid it atop the table nearest the far-left wall. He lifted the lid so as to reveal its contents only to himself, then removed from it a small dark box he put to his right. He began shifting the shape of the box, slivers of it flattening until it formed a dark circle larger than his head.

"A volunteer," he demanded. Tattle raised her hand, the crowd cheered her forward.

"Hold this, love. And fear nothing but the hand of God."

Tattle held up the sphere directly in front of her face. Pritchett yanked a blindfold from his pocket and affixed it to her face.

Pritchett stood a short distance back and pulled out a knife, which he demonstrated to the crowd. As he tossed it across the suitcase, it disappeared into a puff of smoke, and a pigeon flew into the air. The crowd clapped.

"What's all that about?" asked Tattle.

"Never you mind, dear. Merely devilish conjurings."

"That was a new one," Celia said to Colm. "Sort of. The bird living was a novelty, anyway. He's a fiend in that way."

Pritchett performed a few guessing games with the

audience, cards and pocket objects he'd gleaned from earlier observations. A rabbit miraculously doubled as it passed through a looking glass, again crossing over the case. He closed with a bullet catch, Lausanne operated the handgun. When the powder blew and Pritchett demonstrated the slug to the crowd, they applauded. Closing his suitcase, the locals thronged him.

Colm decided the bullet catch tomorrow would be the time to do it. Lausanne would be occupied, he'd only have to contend with Ribbon if they saw what he was doing. Set the fire, apprehend Celia in the chaos, bind her across Mary and take her to the authorities in Sydney.

As he watched Pritchett's easy dealings with his admirers, Celia surprised him.

"I thought more about what you said. Did you have some place in mind?"

"A spot in the desert. These rocks. It's not anything at all if you'd rather not. We can take a walk or something," Colm said.

"That could be nice."

After the hubbub subsided, Celia and Colm walked along the outskirts of town, while a blood orange sun quaked in the sky above them.

"Seeing him here after seeing him there got me wound up."

"Passage of time and all that."

"There's things I left undone that way."

"Well there's things and then there's things," he said. "If you could leave it, isn't it the sort of thing you should?"

"I didn't really though. It wasn't so much a choice, I mean. I ache sometimes. You're like him."

"The wish of every gentleman calling on a lady, bringing to mind her previous suitor."

"Not just him. The city. You're like the city. Like everything I built. Everything I lost."

"How about a ride to remind you of all that's beautiful around here?"

"Where's your horse?" she asked.

They mounted Mary. Celia gripped Colm's torso, and they rode to the grove of desert oaks facing the rocks. He gathered wood for a fire. They laid on his blanket and gazed at the sky. She fell asleep in his arms. He couldn't bring himself to do it for the first hour, just stared at her face glowing in the light.

When she woke a short time later, she was bound at the wrists and feet.

"What's this?" she asked, like it was some sort of lover's game. He couldn't think of any good way to explain it, so he covered her mouth with his handkerchief to avoid more questions.

He strung her face down across Mary, then mounted the horse and rode towards Sydney. They stayed off the main roads, and never spoke another word to each other.

PART III

Some years previous, Colm found himself in South Africa fighting the Dutch on behalf of Her Majesty. He spent the last few months of the war manning a three-storied stone blockhouse in a desolate portion of grassy highlands with a skeleton crew of khaki-clad privates under a stiff-lipped lieutenant named Rohmer.

The structure was built alongside a rail line fenced with razor wire, which the few remaining rebels relentlessly clipped before blowing sections of the tracks to bits. Colm had twice accompanied a convoy of engineers tasked with restringing the enclosure and repairing the demolished line, and on a third occasion, helped to reconstitute a station house which had been dynamited into rubble. Despite these tantrums, the war was winding down. Rumors passed through of his regiment's reassignment to Aden in the coming weeks.

He often pulled watch duty with the dark-haired, short-tempered Haskard, the son of a cobbler from Donegal. While combing the fields for non-existent militants, they devised a far-ranging game of sackcloth and hay scarecrows, hidden by the other, whose capture accumulated an endless tally of points. Colm greatly preferred these amusements to the rear duty his regiment performed in the early months of the conflict, where the endless sniping of hidden adversaries had halved their number.

It was during this final lapse in calamitous activity, while Colm was conducting nighttime vigilance from the third-floor observation deck of the blockhouse, that the priest named Abraham Van Zijl entered his life. Amidst a light drizzle beyond the loophole, Colm spotted two figures in black suits stumbling through the field. Colm alerted Haskard, who had dozed off with a novel on his chest. They trained their Lee-Metfords on the figures.

"Wounded. No rifles," said Haskard.

They climbed the ladder to the floor below, where the other six privates and their lieutenant were asleep on metal cots pressed against the wall. Upon rousing the men, Colm and Haskard slipped through the blockhouse entrance, and clambered atop the stone wall that surrounded it, finding the intruders again with their rifles.

The taller one, with the thick dark beard and sleepy eyes, looked up at the observers.

"We are simply missionaries," he said. "The Boers fell upon our wagon outside of Bloemfontein."

Colm motioned for the men to approach the wall. Haskard crossed the iron threshold in the stone barricade and checked the men for weapons. He shook his head, then took a closer look at the blossom of red in the bald man's wounded stomach.

"Come on then," he said, leading the travelers into the blockhouse.

Shortly after they'd laid the man flat within the quarters, he died. The rain abated with dawn, whereupon they carried him outside and dug a grave down the back hillside.

Van Zijl spoke a few words over the dirt in German, made the sign of the cross, and the coterie marched towards the blockhouse. Colm stopped Rohmer, noting the precise mustache atop his sinewy face had greyed at some point.

"Sir, do we think they were passing messages for the rebels?"

"The war's done, private."

As the men shared a stew atop the long wooden table near their cots, Rohmer asked Van Zijl of his plans.

"I'm venturing to Cape Town," he said. "Would you have a horse to spare?"

"None we could lose permanently. A few of my men can escort you to the train station and then bring it back."

"Might I request the two who granted us their mercy?"

Rohmer nodded, at which point, the other privates began volleying a list of demands their two representatives needed to obtain from the stores in town.

The next morning, the three men set out on horseback across the veld, waving every few miles to their compatriots at the adjoining blockhouses.

Haskard passed one of his hand-rolled cigarettes to Colm, then offered one to Van Zijl, who shook his head.

"How long were you in Johannesburg?" Colm asked.

"Almost the whole war. I meant to leave sooner, but the preacher I was visiting took ill, and in his absence, I became a little too involved in local affairs."

They arrived at the station, a slope of corrugated iron over stone, which bordered a handful of similarly constructed stores. Beside them, train tracks threaded through hills which repeated into a hazy nothingness ahead.

"If you find yourself in Cape Town and in need of a friendly ear, I preach at Last Redeemer."

They said their goodbyes, and Colm hardly thought of the man in the years that followed.

After the debacles in Australia a decade later, Colm boarded a steamship to London. Engine trouble delayed it in Cape Town. Gazing at the majestic hulk of Table Mountain looming over the city's stone and corrugated iron buildings like an angry shadow, he decided to spend a few weeks exploring its sinister crevices.

He chose one of the more sordid hotels in District Six, just beyond the docks, in an area populated by gambling dens and whorehouses. Across the room from his dusty bed was a decaying armoire where he planted his haversack. To the bed's right, a window overlooked a waterlogged alley. Passing the front desk, he bid adieu to the spectacled Polish hotelier in the tattered gray clawhammer coat and commenced a weeks-long study in self-destruction.

After a particularly debaucherous evening in a smoke-filled cantina, Colm woke up in an alleyway on an unfamiliar street. He stood, vomited, then wended through a few residential blocks until he found the familiar, crowded commerce of Hanover Street.

Across the thoroughfare was a simple, drab chapel, a marker in front of it chiseled: 'Last Redeemer.'

Colm walked through the open doors and took in the austerity of the wooden pews and pulpit. Sitting in a back row, thumbing through a bible, was Van Zijl. Colm sat down beside him.

Van Zijl inspected Colm for a moment before finally recognizing him.

"What has brought you here, my friend?"

"I needed a place to sit down. How have the years treated you?"

"Kinder than most," he said. "Are you in a similar line of work these days?"

"Similar methods anyway," Colm said.

"They would prove useful around here."

"For anyone in particular?"

Van Zijl suppressed something painful with his smile.

"I can help," Colm said.

"Let's take a meal first," said Van Zijl.

The priest locked the chapel, then led Colm through its rear entrance to a corrugated shack. Its bleak insides were split between a bedroom, and a small kitchen, where they ate bread and sliced oxen atop a wobbly wooden table.

"I have a niece who has fallen prey to a bad sort," Van Zijl explained. "She is being misused regularly by a man named Horace Grimmley. He won't hear of her release, and she is too under his sway to revolt."

"Perhaps it's better left untouched."

"The man is demonic. The last woman he took for a wife is laid up in an asylum, raving. I can pay for her release," Van Zijl explained. "But one or both parties need to be convinced first."

"I'll ask about it."

Van Zijl gave the address of the brothel, which was a few blocks away.

Colm went back to his hotel, washed and changed, then ventured off to rescue the damsel.

The brothel was another simple, gray stone building. Within, dimly lit by orange gas lamps festooning the walls, a filthy red-haired bartender stood behind an uneven counter. He motioned Colm to a seat in front of him before pouring the gin.

"I'd like some company," said Colm. "I've heard good things about Miriam."

"She's around," said the bartender.

Colm paid his coin, then followed a dark corridor to the left, up a staircase to a hallway of rooms. He entered the one humming amber light below the doorway.

Seated at a desk in front of a mirror, the young woman in the dark blue dress with red flowers combed her blonde hair as a phonograph spun a festive orchestral tune beside her. She had a sly, knowing grin, and confidently rearranged herself to face Colm as he entered.

"Early in the day, isn't it?"

"It is," he said. "How do you like it here?"

"The fuck's that matter?" she asked.

"I prefer happy whores," he said.

"I prefer johns that mind their own fucking business."

Colm smiled, then left.

He stayed at the bar for another drink, and as he was finishing it, Grimmley entered. He had short silver hair, and penetrating eyes over a well-cropped beard, all complemented by a neat, blue suit.

"You're finding the establishment to your satisfaction," Grimmley said as he leaned against the bar.

"Quite," said Colm.

"Of whom did he partake?" Grimmley asked the bartender.

"Miriam," he replied.

"She is sensational, no?"

Colm nodded.

"Is there another proclivity we might accommodate?"

"Such as?"

Grimmley studied Colm's face, then opened his eyes wide with some obscure discovery.

"There's the problem. We're talking about the wrong things," Grimmley decided.

Grimmley eased serpentine into the seat beside him. He had the bartender pour them two more gins.

"I have been deprived of property, which strictly speaking, I am not allowed to possess. And I am currently embroiled in other local affairs which have tied up the resources I normally would have used to obtain my just due. Someone might affect my recompense."

"What would someone be recovering?"

"Diamonds. To the man in question, they mean nothing. To me, they are everything."

Grimmley wrote down an address on a piece of paper, and slid it over to Colm.

"The man in question will be occupied at a social event in two nights, with the only person he suspects would be brazen enough to do him wrong."

"You."

"This is correct. There is a safe welded into the floor beneath a desk on the second level. Whatever else you find is yours."

Colm returned to his hotel and slept until the next morning. He went to the address on the paper, and took a look at the two-story, whitewashed residential building in question. He examined the surrounding area to his satisfaction before going back to his room.

The next evening, he returned. There was only darkness within, no sounds. He pried the door open with his knife, then casually walked through the pitch-black living room. All the furniture was cloaked in canvas. He walked up the noisy stairs. He found the safe beneath a gaudy floral rug after a few moments of fumbling beneath the oak desk. He laid his ear to it, cracked the lock, then put the leather satchel with the diamonds in his coat.

He was back at Grimmley's bar within an hour.

He drank himself into a stupor. At some point, Miriam had joined him, and was nursing a whiskey to his right.

"How about we try that whole business again," Colm slurred out.

Miriam shrugged her shoulders, then led him to her room.

When they were through, Colm lit a cigarette. He was about halfway through it when she spoke.

"You need to leave," she said. Colm put on his clothes and went to the bar.

When Grimmley arrived, he took a seat next to Colm, who calmly slid the satchel over to him.

Grimmley checked the contents. He delicately split out a portion of the diamonds, then grazed them across the tabletop. Colm placed the cut in his jacket.

"How long will you remain here?" asked Grimmley. "Perhaps I'll need you again."

"Maybe I'll be back then," he said, patting Grimmley on the shoulder before he left.

The next morning, Colm stumbled to Van Zijl's shack. There, he found the old man sitting in the dirt beyond its entry, struggling to affix a new table leg to its vacant rim.

Van Zijl's eyes flickered with hope as they met Colm's. "You spoke to them?"

"I did. I just wanted to do you the courtesy of a response. Whoever you knew, she's not that girl anymore."

Van Zijl nodded, his sad eyes and filthy hands returning to his new experiment in frustration.

Colm lugged his own aching frame to the hotel room, gathered his haversack, and boarded the next ship to the Commonwealth.

PART IV

The steamer from London to Tierra del Fuego was christened the Nuncio. It was operated by a Portuguese brigand turned capitalist named Vasquez de Alhambra who was barred from half the ports in Europe. Its inward leg had deposited the seasonal wool output of an estancia run by a Rye Flemyng, who owned 10 square miles of property south of Argentina's Rio Grande, into the hands of London merchants with unclear, but serious, ties to Colm's enquiry service.

At the behest of his beloved Clotilde, Colm was to become embroiled in a seemingly innocuous property dispute lying in stalemate due to Mr. Flemyng's refusal to communicate with a distant relation. Said relation wished to sell off a parcel of Scottish farmland with unfavorable taxation, an action requiring Flemyng's approval. It seemed to Colm a ridiculous reason to embark on the lengthy sea voyage across the Atlantic, and yet, the Men Upstairs had decided just that.

There was no jetty along the shore, the steamer embanked directly onto the beach. There, via metal plank, Indian workers from the nearby farms off-loaded cargo containers onto covered ox-drawn carts. Afterwards, they disappeared into the ramshackle of white wood buildings that lined the inlet, or the dirt roads to the interior forests, themselves dwarfed by snow-drenched mountains carving through a blue haze of atmosphere. Among the workers was Colm's escort, led by a young, lithe Ona Indian named Cyprian, who wore a white cotton tunic along with dark pants and boots.

He was accompanied by two other natives in similar garb. Benedict was short-haired, small and stumpy, and wore a blue vest over his shirt. Tikhon was of average height with gangly limbs, and his hair was tied back in a ponytail. Cyprian waved Colm over, introduced the group, and they loaded the final few crates onto the wagon before setting off down the road to Flemyng's estate.

They passed two other properties on the way. The first was a slight, fenced-in bit of woodlands on a hillside, within which scattered sheep sauntered through a screen of trees. It was run by an old man named Farrier said to be an escaped convict from Ushuaia Prison, but whom Cyprian spoke of fondly.

As the road corked south, they passed an unassuming edge of the Tertullian estate, endless forest interrupted by a bog. Cyprian explained the actual grounds comprised something like 150 square miles ceded by the government as a political favor. Within a few hours, they were at the Flemyng property, crossing the wooden gate of its threshold into a flat field of roaming sheep being tended by another genial, long-haired Indian in tan garments named Sabas, whom Flemyng had adopted some years previous.

Sabas broke apart from the flock, shook Colm's hand, and the group ventured along the dirt road to a half dozen white buildings with dark red roofs. The men led the oxen into one of the storage buildings and off-loaded the crates while Colm walked over to the main house. He stepped onto the veranda, knocked on the door, and Flemyng greeted him. He was a large, jolly man with brown hair. He wore suspenders over a fraying red shirt, along with black pants and boots filthy with clay.

He shook Colm's hand, and invited him inside the kitchen, which fringed the central staircase of the anteroom. The wife, Annemarie, was an older woman in a dark brown dress, with dirty-blonde hair and a slightly mischievous smirk. She was laying out tea and meat and bread on the large wooden table in front of the black stove that dominated that back portion of the room.

Their teenage son was seated at the table, reading a weathered adventure novel. His name was Fletcher, and he was a tiny repetition of his father, including his clothing, though he possessed an added air of self-seriousness. After their introductions, Colm took the seat in front of him. Fletcher stared ahead with guarded fascination.

"You've come from London?"

"Most recently," said Colm, downing his tea.

"Haven't been since I was little. For a funeral, was it?" Fletcher asked his mom.

"That's right," Annemarie said. "Your great aunt."

Fletcher nodded, both seemed proud of him for remembering.

"We'll be back there once you're well again," she said.

"There was an outbreak of smallpox last spring," Flemyng explained. "Claimed a few of the natives. Did a number on the boy here, immunity be damned."

Colm nodded as he finished off his portion of oxen.

"Savory," Colm said. "The food, not your misfortunes."

"They're one and the same to someone," Flemyng replied.

"Not to the men who have sent me."

"Very well, undo my suspicions on the veranda."

Colm and Flemyng walked onto the porch, sitting down in two wooden chairs overlooking the field that joined the forest ahead. Flemyng produced two cigars, lit them, then handed one to Colm.

"It's simple paperwork," said Colm.

"We've an agreement, going years back. To make hell for one another," said Flemyng.

"I think he's grown weary of it."

"Ten years ago, he would have sent a band of cutthroats to burn down these buildings. And now, you in their place."

"You'd prefer a fight?"

"Of course not. I mourn the spirit we've lost. The one that yearned. I'll send the papers back with you."

They smoked down the cigars, watching Sabas lugging one of the new crates to a different building. Flemyng examined Colm before he spoke again.

"You've spent some time in the brush."

Colm nodded.

"There's one thing I require before acceding to that barbarian's demands," said Flemyng. "Something I can't spare any of my people for, which is just as well, as it's likely a doomed enterprise."

"Then I am your man, Mr. Flemyng."

"Lost a boy last spring. Took off after his sweetheart. Into the mountains. Any other time, I would've hired one of the Indians to get him, but we can't spare any hands. Even to find a tracker."

"What's his name?"

"Erasmus."

"He steal from you?"

"No. He had something of a reputation."

"At cards?"

"Shearing. He could clear 300 head of sheep a day, no problem. One of the men from the other properties is organizing a competition, and he wants to unseat the champion."

Colm laughed.

"Quite ridiculous, isn't it?" Flemyng asked.

"I'll do my best to find him," said Colm.

"Excellent. There's a spare bed in the workers' quarters that way. Breakfast before dawn."

Colm grabbed his haversack, then walked to the rickety wooden building beyond all the rest.

Tikhon, Cyprian and Benedict were playing cards within, at a lantern-lit table surrounded by bunk beds. Colm dropped his belongings on one of the spare mattresses, then dragged a chair over to the table to be dealt in.

"I'm to find your missing companion, Erasmus. Do you gentlemen have any leads?"

They shook their heads and played the next few hands in silence.

"We know where he is," Cyprian finally admitted.

"Why not tell the old man?" asked Colm.

"It would have been a betrayal of sorts. He asked for solitude. We assumed he'd be back by now."

"Then let me find him and put your worries at ease."

"There's a moor beyond a ridge of mountains to the north and west of here. He meant to build a shelter there for his bride."

The next morning, Colm ate breakfast with the workers, then Sabas gave him a few days' worth of supplies and an angry mule named Seymour from the corral. Sabas gestured the path through the woodlands to the bluish mountains elevating to the north and west, and Colm set off towards them.

It was a day's ride through thick forest. He crossed two small streams before he got to the edge of the mountains. There, he followed a guanaco trail up the side of the elevation. Passing through a slit in the rocks, he found a valley down below. The right half was forest, the left half was composed of flatlands spattered with small bodies of water and overgrown heath. The valley rose in the distance into clay-covered hills that stuttered into faraway fog.

Where the forest met the flatlands, there was a small wooden shack, with scattered sheep wandering nearby. Colm rode Seymour down below.

On Colm's approach, the Indian they called Erasmus

appeared from within the shack. He had sad eyes, a thick beard, and graying black hair. He was wearing a brown tunic over black pants and boots. Colm stopped a healthy interval away, waving his empty hands. Erasmus nodded, then Colm approached.

"Flemyng sent you?"

"He did."

The door to the shack opened and the wife appeared. She had dark circles around her haunted eyes, long brown hair and a shawl of guanaco fur over her blue dress. Her battered bare knees showed over dirty brown boots.

"This is Clementine," Erasmus said. Colm waved at her, and Clementine tilted her head suspiciously. "What does Flemyng want?"

"They're organizing a contest on the farm."

"Hortensio," said Erasmus. "Looking to win back his title."

"Flemyng will make good on any reasonable demands."

Erasmus looked at the shack and the surrounding property.

"I may have some."

Erasmus kissed his wife, found a spare mule that had strayed into the woods, and then the two men started the journey through the mountains. They camped overnight in the forest at the foot of the incline and made it back to Flemyng's farm the next morning.

There was an air of celebration in the worker's quarters as Erasmus became reacquainted with his companions, but they could sense his reticence, and understood it to be a temporary reunion.

Colm found Flemyng in the main house, and secured the last of the paperwork before dinner that evening, along with Flemyng's promise to cable an official notice to London before the end of the week. The next merchant steamer to the Falklands, where Colm would arrange transport to Europe, wouldn't arrive for another few days, so he allowed himself to get swept up in the excitement of the coming conflict.

It was being arranged by the esteemed Tertullian family for the following Saturday, and all of Flemyng's men were invited. They spruced themselves up as best they could in clean tunics and pants with greased down hair, and by oxen cart made the journey just after sunrise that morning. Flemyng was talked into attending as a formality, but his wife and two sons remained behind, citing a need for vigilance in the wake of recent larceny. However, Cyprian vaguely alluded to an incident the previous year that had strained relations between the two families.

The oxen carts wended through wooden gates leading up a hillside of trees towards the Tertullian estate, comprised of twice as many buildings as Flemyng's property and of similar composition, but all painted a light blue. Beyond the two rows of buildings were meticulous fences wherein roamed hundreds of sheep in a pasture that bordered yet another forest.

To the buildings' left were two massive, gaudy canvas tents, outside of which, drunken workers lingered or caroused. Flemyng's men, first checking their concealed armaments, dismounted, tying their oxen off in a vacant corral beside the buildings before they entered the larger tent en masse.

Torches lit the interior red and orange, and there was a small wooden ring constructed in the center with two shearing tables separated by a low wooden divider. Behind the tables were four separate corrals, the center two filled with fifty sheep each. There were wooden benches to the left and right of the ring where the spectators began to take their seats.

Eustace Hortensio, in a clean barber's outfit, ventured onto the right portion of the stage. He was corpulent, with receding red hair, and a pointed mustache. He carried a leather satchel with him, which he unfurled on the table, producing an eloquent set of shears. Erasmus walked onstage, shook hands with Eustace, then from his brown haversack, produced his own well-kept set of equipment. The proceedings were to be decided by the head of the hacienda, Ignatius Tertullian, who entered a few moments later. He was a thin man, with neat gray hair and a matching beard, wearing an eloquent dark frock, with matching black pants and shoes. He was accompanied by his wife and daughter, dark-haired beauties in comely black dresses.

The women took a seat at the back of the tent, while Tertullian walked over to Flemyng and they shared pleasantries. Tertullian then made his way to the stage and greeted both competitors.

Four of Tertullian's workers walked behind the stage, ready to release the first animals at the start of the contest. The crowd that had been hovering outside all took their seats, and the proceedings began.

Tertullian raised a handkerchief, then let it fall to the ground, before stepping outside of the ring. As he did, the workers in back released the first sheep. The men on stage began their artistry, placing the animals on the tables before shearing them delicately, while piles of wool on the floor blossomed. Once an animal was bare, they passed it off to a worker who led the shorn into the vacant stall, while their partner produced a new creature for the combatants.

It was a sweaty, energetic matter, lasting not more than a half hour. The contest remained undecided until the final few minutes, when Erasmus took the lead and won by two head of sheep. The crowd erupted in applause. The men shook hands, and Tertullian approached the stage, clapping until he raised the victor's arm. The noisy horde then ambled into the next tent for the celebration.

There, a feast was assembled on wooden tables, and the men ate their fill and prattled for the remainder of the afternoon. A few hours before darkness descended, Flemyng shook Tertullian's hand, and he and his men found their oxen carts and made the voyage home. Once there, Flemyng gifted Erasmus some corrugated iron and supplies for his farm. Afterwards, he talked the man into coming back to work at the property for a week every month in exchange for shipping Erasmus' wool with his own back to Europe.

Colm boarded the steamer to the Falklands a few days later, somehow reinvigorated by the affair.

PART V

Colm lived in a two-room flat on Hereford Street with yellow walls and a brown carpet. The front room had a stove, a table, two chairs, a kitchen cabinet over a wash basin, a sofa and a bookshelf, as well as a red-curtained window overlooking the street. There was a bed and a desk in the back room, along with a heavy locked trunk containing personal effects. The building was a short walk to the enquiry office on Russell Street. He ventured towards it beneath a gray sky, taking the long route so as to pass by the British Museum. That morning, the eaves above its stone columns drizzled with dwindling morning rain.

The enquiry office was a small brick building with no sign and no distinguishing features. He knocked on its wooden side door, which was partially hidden by rose bushes. After a scampering of footsteps within, the door opened, and he was greeted by the elderly Ms. Clotilde. She had white hair, spectacles adorning her severe face, and a loose white blouse over her gray skirt.

Ms. Clotilde stuck her head past Colm, staring down the alley and across the street at a young woman smoking in a yellow dress beside another office building. The woman smiled. Clotilde returned a forced grin, then she and Colm entered the office.

Brown wood walls surrounded a desk at the far end, bordered by a bookshelf next to a shuttered window. The carpet was gray. There were two doors, one behind her desk that led to the archives, and one against the right wall. Colm knew there was a staircase beyond that one which led to the Men Upstairs.

Clotilde sat behind her desk, then took out a set of cigarettes, offering one to Colm as he sat down in front of her. She placed an ashtray between them, examining him for any subtle changes that might have accrued over the last few months.

"Did the land of fire live up to its name?"

Colm shook his head.

"They've tamed it. What wilds are left are within men."

After they'd each had a few puffs, Clotilde took a brown folder from the top drawer of the desk and pushed it across the counter. Colm opened the envelope and read through her typed notes, which described the disappearance of a munitions factory foreman named Bornley Moldon.

"I'll see to it, then. Hold down the fort, darling." Colm took the folder and left.

The missing man had lived with his wife Helene on Raglan Road. She greeted Colm at the door of their second story apartment. She had curly red hair and wore a loose blue dress. She and Colm drank tea atop a decorative metal table just inside the doorway, while she nervously explained his behavior before the disappearance.

"He'd gotten in with some men who had a notion to change things."

"With extralegal methods?"

"It was spoken of," she said quickly, sipping her tea.

"Where did these men meet?"

She shook her head.

"One of the men he associated with was a playwright

named Gull. He came in once. I believe he left a pamphlet for one of his shows."

She went over to a bookshelf and rifled out the leaflet, which she handed to Colm. It had an address for a West End theater. Colm said he'd be back in touch and went to find the playwright.

The theater was a ragged affair, black brick situated along a row of pubs that were crowded with early afternoon patrons. Within its walls, a few rows of empty dark wood seats angled down to a small, black stage. There was a man lying down in the center, dressed like a renaissance nobleman. He was smoking a cigarette while tearing up pages of a play and tossing them into the seats when Colm entered.

As Colm approached, the man sat up, squinting angrily. He had dark hair, a thin face and menacing eyes. He pulled a flask from his belt and took a swig.

"Are you Frederick Gull?"

"The correct party may address me as such. Are you with the Committee on Morals or whatever the hell it's called?"

"Afraid not."

"Ribaldi sent you for the rent, then?"

"I'm not here for that, either," said Colm.

"Well, out with it then."

"I'd like to speak with you about Moldon."

"The dilettante?"

"The disappeared munitions worker."

"One foot in either world. It did tricks with his mind, I believe," said Gull, stumbling to his feet as Colm reached the stage. Gull walked a few steps, then sat down along the edge of the stage, dangling his legs. Colm remained standing, reflexively grazing his hand against the pistol inside his coat.

"You're an agitator, then? Demonstrations and the like."

"I have ideas some might deem transgressive," said

Gull.

"When was the last time you spoke to him?"

"A week or two past."

"Regarding?"

"Art, culture, politics. We are not some society of assassins, sir."

"There are none among your number with ideas veering beyond demonstrative rebellion?'

"Some believe a word might carve cleaner than a knife," said Gull.

"Some might procure a whetstone and relieve themselves of ridiculous opinions," said Colm. "When is your next performance?"

"Alas, there are those less dedicated to the art form than I, so our coming performance has been delayed."

"Did the workers strike?"

"You are a detective and a jester it seems. I welcome you to investigate the piss-ridden alley outdoors. Take care, sir."

Colm found a seat in a gray-hued pub across the street and watched the entrance of the theater. When it got dark, Gull, now wearing a black coat, exited, locking the door behind him. Colm followed him a mile away to a vertical stack of apartments above a hardware store. Gull remained there for an hour, then ventured out again, traveling a half mile to a white brick pub, where he met a dark-haired man with a beard and spectacles in a black suit. They stayed inside speaking for close to an hour, then went separate directions in front of the establishment. Gull appeared to be returning to his apartment, so Colm followed the second gentleman. About a quarter mile into the pursuit down a desolate street of decaying brick houses, the gentleman turned around.

"We have some business between us?" he asked in an Eastern European accent that Colm couldn't place.

"Do you know a man named Moldon?"

"This is a dark place, friend. In the dark we might do

dreadful things."

"Have you learned this of yourself recently? When you moved the corpse, maybe."

"Would you toy with one so recently practiced?"

"I've never paid two coins when one might do. The widow needs a body."

"You're asking for some manner of betrayal. But one can only burn the kindling in one's hands."

"This offer comes around once."

"So does a threat without a response in kind," said the man, smiling as he turned and left.

Colm made his way back to the theater and forced the lock. Inside, he found a back office possessing little of interest in the steel cabinets surrounding the small desk. He left it in disarray, stifling the urge to set a match as he left. He stood outside the front door in the street, smoking. He finally walked back to Gull's apartment, but the lights were extinguished.

One of Colm's informants in bygone years was a fence who frequented a pub called The Wild Feather near the docks. Bereft of leads, Colm made his way there. It was black brick burning orange within the windows. Inside, dock workers drank atop the bar's wooden counter, or caroused with whores at the circular tables. The man in question was nowhere to be found. Colm was surprised to discover Grimmley, clad in a black suit, had at some point made the voyage from South Africa and posted himself at a table near the staircase in the back right corner of the room.

Grimmley waved him over.

"You've established yourself in the city?" Colm asked.

"I have. You look like you do a different kind of business here."

"I could afford to be uncivilized elsewhere," Colm said, lighting a pair of cigarettes and handing one to Grimmley as he took a seat. "There was a disappearance, probably a murder. Munitions worker."

"The death of a civilian. Truly different business around these parts."

"The men in question were a gangly theater type and a gentleman. Eastern Europe maybe, spectacles. Knew how to handle himself. I figured he might be involved in some other local escapades."

"Indeed, he was. Though not so brazen as to ask about a body, such a gentleman questioned a colleague about procuring a paralyzing agent. When he got a little more comfortable, he let it slip it was on behalf of a known person performing some manner of stunt. He said we'd likely read about it in the papers."

"Could I speak with him?"

"I can telephone him," Grimmley said. He led Colm into a small back room filled with casks of spirits, and a telephone hanging from the wall beside a ladder. When the Australian man on the other end answered, Colm asked about the second gentleman.

"A prickly fella," said the informant. "Came from Prussia or thereabouts. Involved with some nebulous depravity back that way, but sounded like he was making a clean break, investing in the arts. Said his name was Gehrloff."

"Address?"

"Didn't get that familiar, mate."

"Thanks for everything else, anyway."

Colm hung up the phone, said goodbye to Grimmley and went back to his flat. When he woke in the morning, he went back to the theater. Gull was inside, pacing and smoking along the stage again.

"Did I not tell you to fuck off efficiently enough last night?"

"When do you think Gehrloff is going to ask for a favor in return?" asked Colm. "That the sort of man you want to be in debt to? More importantly, do you think it'll stop at one request?"

Gull tossed his cigarette onto the stage and stubbed it

out with his foot. He stared at Colm with a wordless pout.

"I'll be back by later," Colm said, exiting the theater then walking across the street to the pub.

After about an hour, Gull left and Colm followed him down the road. It was a half mile to the brown apartment building Gull disappeared into. Colm waited, but he didn't come out. Colm checked the back of the building, where he found a rusted cart lingering near another doorway, then went back to his hiding spot.

After another hour, Gehrloff emerged by himself. Colm followed him down to another public house, where the European ordered a meal and ate it quickly before returning to the building. Colm lingered around its outskirts until sunset, when he took another spot with a better view of the back entrance. An hour after it got dark, Gehrloff emerged carrying several black bags, which he placed in the cart. He made a single return trip, and emerged again with two more bags, placing them in the cart and disappearing down a darkened alley.

Colm followed Gehrloff into an abandoned industrial structure a few blocks away, where a furnace remained along rows of rubble and destroyed metal. As Gehrloff started to take out the first bag, Colm drew his pistol and approached him.

"Another mistake?" Colm asked.

"Not this one."

"Moldon's death, it was some kind of stunt?"

"Gull wanted him to smuggle out munitions. Some kind of riot as part of an art project, a protest for worker's rights. The chemical was supposed to be a scare tactic after he refused. It went badly."

"I have handcuffs," said Colm, approaching.

"You won't get to use them," Gehrloff said.

As Gehrloff went for his pistol, Colm fired. Gehrloff slumped over the cart, dead. Colm walked over to the bags to verify his suspicion, finding chunks of Gull's hacked up body within.

Colm left the scene intact, locating the local constable, explaining the situation, then leading him back to the scene. When they were done, he phoned Clotilde from the police station.

The following day, Colm went to Moldon's apartment, telling the widow what happened with as much delicacy as he could. She wept as Colm held her. Afterwards, he returned to his apartment and fell asleep.

PART VI

Colm was wandering through the West End a few nights later when he came across the puppeteer. A crowd had gathered, laughing on a street corner beside a closed down garment store. He edged his way in, and saw a box draped in black velvet, with a kind old man's head peeking up behind it. A severe widow's peak interrupted his long grey hair, and he wore a bright yellow suit. Within the box, two artfully cut wooden dolls dressed as red cloaked monarchs danced before a woodland scene. Their master mouthed a comedy where two nobles paired their ill-tempered offspring to unite a war-torn kingdom. At the end of the short scene, the crowd erupted in joyful applause. Colm smiled at the old man and tossed a few shillings in the bowler hat beside the box.

Colm returned the next evening, enjoying a brief reprise of the material before he was on his way again. Not seeing the old man a few nights later, he didn't think much of it. But on his way back along the street that same night, he found a younger man had taken his place. This man had thick dark hair primped up, and wore a suit made entirely of blue velvet.

His voice was deeper, his two, gold-cloaked puppets

more sardonic, tricksters. They hatched a horrifying plan to overthrow a kingdom through a series of murders that cleared the line of succession. At the end, the crowd cackled. When the audience left, Colm talked to the new puppeteer.

"An interesting show."

The young puppeteer shrugged his shoulders.

"What happened to the old man who was here a few nights ago?"

"Couldn't tell you, friend," he said in a gravelly voice. "People come and go."

As the young puppeteer was packing up his trunk, Colm caught sight of a devious wooden face embedded in gold cloth within.

"Part of the show I missed?"

"Let the mystery fuel your anticipation for the next performance."

The puppeteer left and Colm went about his business.

As Colm was returning home from the Wild Feather a few weeks later, he took a shortcut through a fog-drenched block of abandoned warehouses. When he passed one of the establishments, he thought he recognized a voice within.

He stepped into the threshold of the doorway. The room was almost entirely cleared out, just a few bits of broken machinery were strewn against the walls. There was a row of support posts along the center of the room, and behind one, there was a dark red container. It threw orange light onto the back wall, and smoke seemed to pour from it.

As Colm approached, he kept one hand on his pistol.

When he rounded the container, he saw the old puppeteer lying in a pile of tattered robes in front of a fire, drinking a bottle of whiskey. His box and puppets were missing.

"Where are your friends?"

"Waiting for me," the puppeteer said, gesturing to the

fire.

"There's a cheap boarding house nearby," said Colm.

Colm lifted the old man to his feet, then they walked a few blocks to a slovenly establishment. It was run by a brown-haired madam in a black dress, who smoked behind a wooden counter. Colm set the man up for a week in a small downstairs room and promised to return in the morning.

After a night's sleep back at Hereford, he returned to the boarding house. He knocked on the puppeteer's door but received no answer. He returned with the madam, who unlocked the room. They found the window open, and the bed vacated, save for a spot of blood that led to the windowsill.

Colm looked out the window and saw the blood spatter continue into the alley and then disappear. He checked the bed quickly before the madam forced him to leave, discovering a splintered fragment of a devious doll face. Colm pocketed the clue and left.

He recalled a doll shop less than a mile away from the location, and ventured into its bright red, puppet-festooned walls, where he found a middle-aged clerk who eyed the remnant carefully.

"The older puppeteer was a regular fixture around here years ago. Aeschylus. When he returned from America, everything had changed, including his fortunes. The younger man sounds like Boccaccio. He claimed to have come from Italy, but his accent was inconsistent at best. I'd guess Liverpool."

"Was Boccaccio what you'd call a nefarious sort?"

"I never did like him, but that's hardly cause to hang a man."

"Does he do any regular shows around here?"

"At a tavern nearby. The Last Switch."

Colm found the tavern that night, small sturdy wood humming yellow within. Two dozen drunkards were inside, most ignoring the man at the far side of the room performing the puppet act. Colm ordered a drink and watched the show from the bar.

Boccaccio seemed tense and gloomy. Halfway through the performance, sweat dripping down his face, he lost his words, and stared into a vacancy ahead of him. He was awoken from his trance by a thrown tomato.

Boccaccio wiped the tomato from his face and finished the show. Afterwards, he got into a muffled argument with the bartender. He grabbed his box of coins and his trunk of puppets, then stormed out of the building. Colm was waiting for him a few steps from the door.

He said nothing, just held up the fragment of the doll face he'd found on the bed.

"I've never been able to get it right," Boccaccio explained. "The design, the way he showed me when I was younger. He found fault in that one too. I smashed it to bits in the room."

"Where is he?"

"Follow me," Boccaccio said.

Colm walked behind Boccaccio down another alleyway, into the back entrance of an abandoned building, lit by a circle of candles. The candles surrounded a massive wooden box. Within, Aeschylus was dressed in a red cloak, his hands strung by rope to the rafters atop the woodlands scene that mimicked his marionette theater.

"Will they hang me?" asked Boccaccio. "Fratricide, isn't it?"

"Yes," said Colm.

"Very well then."

Boccaccio laid his belongings on the ground, then held his hands in front of his body. Colm tied them with rope. They walked to the police station.

PART VII

A few weeks later Colm went to the enquiry office and shared a cup of coffee with Clotilde, who was that day wearing a fine yellow dress with white flowers.

"You'll enjoy this next one," she said, pushing the brown envelope forward.

Colm thumbed through the material.

"I'll be taking the train to the countryside, then."

The next case was to be found at an abandoned castle near the coast. Colm took a coach there from the nearest station. The horse-drawn carriage passed through darkened woods rife with aching bird calls, eventually arriving at a dirt road at the foot of a hill. There, the driver refused to continue, despite Colm's insistence.

"You'll pass over another set of hills that way, then a rickety bridge," the driver said in a thick Scottish accent. "Beyond that, the remains of the castle linger on the coastline."

The driver ventured back through the woods. Colm grabbed his haversack, then ascended the dirt road along the hill, which indeed settled into a pattern of rolling grasslands, misted by the looming coast. As Colm passed over the bridge in question, twenty feet above the curling stream below, the ruins of the castle materialized through the haze. There remained half a curtain wall of crumbled stone, and one tower still standing along its perimeter. Within, the keep was the only structure retaining recognizable shape. Although the top half had been blown off, Colm suspected the ground level and lower chambers might still be in use.

Much nearer to Colm was a fire beside a small wooden shack outside the castle itself. As Colm got near it, he saw a wiry, bearded old man in brown rags. He was sitting on a crate and grilling fish over the flames.

"You tend to this place?" asked Colm.

"What can be done for it," said the old man in a whispery, measured voice. "Take a seat."

Colm grabbed another crate from beside the shack and sat down beside him. The old man cut away portions of fish for Colm into a tin plate.

"What's your name?"

"Perugia," said the old man. Colm gave his as the man handed him the plate.

"We were given limited information about this Countess Moruzi. Is she Italian?"

"Moldavian," said the old man. "Supposedly. I looked after the family she married into. The Vollenhovens. Klaus was her husband's name. The same as his father's and grandfather's."

"You looked after them here?"

Perugia shook his head.

"An estate outside of Birmingham. This ruin belonged to the family for centuries, but as a curiosity. She ventured this way in her madness."

"And you followed?"

"Where else was there to go?" asked Perugia, as though Colm were some conspirator in these ancient events.

"She resides within?"

"She wanders there, yes. I do what I can to ease her savagery. But she lingers in old mysteries."

"Such as the letter alluded to."

"The blood curse, yes. A violence she blames for the downfall of her husband, the death of her children. An unsolved murder that returned to demolish what remained of the unblemished. A century and a half past, Klaus' family was involved in the French violence, the Revolution. They fled to this place. They were safe for a time. At some point in the isolation of winter, they were murdered. Klaus, his wife, his servants, everyone but the last child, the father of my master. He was too young to have carried out such acts, yet it was suspected he harbored some demon within. The child never returned here, nor the child's son, my master, Klaus III. That all changed once my master married Countess Moruzi and had a son himself. On a lark, they dined in the shadows of the castle. Upon venturing back to civilization, my master and his child fell ill with fever and died. Countess Moruzi roamed Europe for a time, but returned here, vowing that if she could not undo the curse, she might at least understand its mystery."

"You have sought answers yourself?"

"It was not for me to do," said Perugia.

"Might I speak to the Countess?"

"That is not for me to say."

"Any other sage words before I begin?"

"I would wait until morning," said Perugia.

Colm slept against the wall inside Perugia's shack.

The next morning, they ate what was left of the fish. Perugia grabbed a wooden fishing pole and walked to the stream near the woods to replenish their supplies while Colm went to explore the ruins.

Colm passed the stone curtain, examining the rubble in the courtyard where the livery and blacksmith's quarters used to be. The threshold to the keep itself had been pried away at some point.

Colm grabbed his lantern from his haversack, lit it with a match, then entered the darkened keep.

The bottom steps of a central staircase were partially visible through the rubble of the collapsed ceiling. The only way forward was by turning left down a corridor, which was just slightly taller than Colm.

Orange light hummed from a wall sconce ahead, Colm walked towards it. Despite the scattered stone along the floor, he could maneuver through most of the hallway. There was an open passage on the left, the door itself broken off the hinges and lying on the floor.

Stepping over it, he found himself in what was probably a music room, ransacked of all valuables. Its purpose was only gleaned upon discovering broken bits of violin amidst the wreckage. As Colm was removing rocks to discover clues, the Countess Moruzi scuttled into the room behind him.

"You are looking for their ghosts below the rubble?"

Colm turned to look at the woman, the raggedy brown dress over her small frame, her filthy long black hair. She possessed the gleaming eyes of a mystic, and her almost serpentine movements made her seem removed from the reality Colm was currently experiencing.

"For anything of note."

"Were you called for, or pillaging of your own accord?"

"The former," he said.

"Steiner, they said."

"They did," said Colm.

Moruzi flitted through the rubble, encircling Colm, examining him.

"Though little is left, much remains. You understand?"

Colm nodded.

"Do you humor me, or do you understand?"

"Would you show me the other rooms? Those permitting access."

Moruzi scampered away from Colm and down the hall to the left. He nearly lost her in the darkness. She turned right ahead and slammed herself against a door until it gave. Colm followed her noises into the room.

Within, the chapel mostly remained. The shattered stained-glass windows on the left cast sunlight onto the pews and simple dais at the front of the room.

"Is there something here we've missed?" she whispered. Colm began looking around, finding nothing of immediate interest.

"I'll be thorough," he assured her. She took a seat at a pew as he continued his search of every crevice within the area. "Does anything else remain?"

Moruzi led Colm out of the chapel, into the darkened interior corridor, where they found a stairwell to the cellars. Moruzi guided Colm through two large dark rooms filled with broken casks. He inspected the walls, the floor, and the wreckage, and found little remained of the past.

"There is one more place, of course," Moruzi said.

They ascended the stairs and left through the front entrance. Colm followed Moruzi along a dirt path behind the keep. They stepped over a portion of demolished wall that had fallen out of true, to the single row of remaining gravestones.

"It is sacrilege, is it not?" she asked Colm.

"But in your estimation, it would absolve his soul," Colm said. "Finding no link below between the man and the atrocity."

"I see it that way."

"Then we will inter them afterwards with prayers."

Colm walked to Perugia's shack, found a shovel, and returned to the gravestone marked Klaus I. He conferred with Moruzi one final time before he started digging. He took a break halfway, his clothes soaked through with sweat. During this repose, Perugia walked over with another shovel to help him finish. It was nearly dark by the time they were done. Colm lit his lantern on the lip of the grave, then used the shovel to pry open the old man's casket.

Clutched in the skeleton's hand was a heart-shaped locket, engraved with the name Anita. Colm handed the locket to Moruzi.

"That's not his wife's name," she said.

"Who is she?"

"A court harlot," Perugia said. "She ended up marrying a duke. Rumors placed her briefly with your husband's grandfather."

"This is beginning to paint an uglier picture," commented Colm. "Let's not disturb the other graves, it seems their loved one may have done enough of that."

Colm inspected the casket one last time, then the two men filled the hole in with dirt. All three made perfunctory signs of the cross, then walked over to Perugia's hut.

They sat around the campfire, consuming salted fish and coffee, and reconstructing what Colm thought was the likeliest scenario.

"This mistress, Anita, might have been the sort of woman with demands," Colm concluded. "With other options, and no desire to settle into a situation where her position was in question. Klaus was perhaps mad with desire. Maybe he and his wife were quarreling anyway, and he saw an opportunity to wipe the past clean. Begin anew."

"Perhaps," said Moruzi, struggling with the unpleasantness of the scenario.

"We can continue rummaging through what remains if you'd like."

"That's quite all right," said Moruzi. "Who could stand another messy knot in such a tale."

The next morning, a dour Moruzi forced a smile as she handed Colm a leather purse with the rest of his payment. He waved goodbye to Perugia, then set off towards the train station.

PART VIII

A few months later, Colm stood amongst the crowd gathered in front of parliament as war was declared against Germany. The morning after, he found the recruitment offices for his old unit, and was in France a few weeks later after a cursory training period for the old-timers.

His term in the trenches was brief and compared unfavorably with his days in Africa. He had spent the early part of the Boer War tracking militants across expansive velds. Even his stretch in the blockhouse, punctuated by periods of violent intensity, hadn't prepared him for the low-burn tension in between skirmishes in France. The trenches, looming walls of filth which enclosed herds of men scurrying like trapped animals, took on a hallucinatory nightmare quality. The sight of soldiers suffocating after the first gas attack from the Germans had a particularly sinister effect on his psyche, and he often woke gasping for air from phantom attacks.

An elaborate plan to capture a town on the Germans' flank spelled his company's demise. Their orders were to cross no-man's-land after a gas strike, but their artillery had malfunctioned, and the Germans began a wholesale slaughter of the intruders. Upon a chaotic retreat, they found themselves caught between the German trench and their own razor wire. A strafing action from a machine gun nest killed most of the men, blew off half of Colm's left hand and shattered his right thigh. He was hours amongst the corpse pile before a relief party provided enough cover for the survivors to retreat into the trench.

He spent a few weeks in a field hospital in France and was then shipped back to London.

PART IX

Colm spent his London convalescence in a morbid mood. Clotilde visited him in the hospital, bringing tea and pulp novels, hinting at lurid developments in the city which had transpired in his absence. Apparently, his friend Grimmley's criminal enterprises were in jeopardy, as upstarts were attempting to take advantage of shifting conditions in the city.

"A whole new class of ruffian these days," she said. "The world's gone mad with the war."

When they released Colm, he was a few fingers lighter and had a limp which necessitated a hickory walking stick. Thankfully the Germans had spared his gun hand, so he saw no problem in returning to his old job. Clotilde, however, claimed the Men Upstairs wanted to make sure he was fully recovered before taking on any new cases.

It was another few weeks into this extended hiatus before he visited the Wild Feather. There, he found Grimmley, himself more haggard, smoking in his favorite spot by the staircase. Grimmley tapped the table, and the red-headed male bartender poured two gins. Colm grabbed them, then took a seat beside Grimmley, who was watching the foot traffic not entering the door.

They finished the drinks in silence, and the bartender walked two more over to them.

"They've been giving you trouble around here?" asked Colm.

"Things are changing. Things always change," he said, reiterating the point like an ancient conversation replaying in his head.

"How are they changing now?"

"As you might expect, there was a labor shortage with the war. I began employing men I was unfamiliar with. Men with other designs."

"The protection rackets, the prostitution..."

"The muscle for it, yes. A few years back, the temperance movement won over some portions of Scotland. We began off-loading product along the coast for some of their dry counties and developed relationships there. Some of our new friends arrived in London shortly after the war to aid in the other businesses."

"These friends have since developed a foothold and begun questioning their prior relationships," Colm guessed.

Grimmley nodded and drained the last of his gin.

"A man named Vasarely worked his way up in the distillery. I'd lost interest in the day-to-day a long time ago..."

"And he's lost interest in tribute."

"There will be a general mutiny among the other businesses. The bookies, the brothels."

"You seem resigned to the loss."

"A retaliation would be pointless. I'd like to broker a final deal. Return to Cape Town, perhaps."

"If it's all coming to an end, I suppose I wouldn't mind seeing you leave the city upright, at least. Where does he do business?"

Grimmley gave the address, a pub near the docks.

"You'll know their answer by the fisherman's haul, I suppose," Colm said, exiting.

Colm found Vasarely's pub that evening. It was a raucous den of white brick. A gaggle of smoking prostitutes in furs leaned against the facade, eyeing Colm as he entered. Within, ornate silver chandeliers formed a tapestry of a ceiling, a spider's web above the crowded, dust-strewn room. A red-headed woman in a dark blouse was tending bar. Two stocky bald men in suits on either side of the room watched Colm approach her.

"Vasarely in here, tonight?" Colm asked her. "I'm here on behalf of Grimmley."

The woman motioned one of the bald men over. He patted Colm down and led him into a back room opposite the front entrance. A standing lamp threw yellow across the desk where Vasarely was squaring bets in a book. He had a shock of orange hair, a sharp face, and was wearing a vest over a white dress shirt. He put his pencil down, his impatient eyes demanding an answer from Colm.

"Grimmley sent me."

"You don't look much for raising hell."

"Not these days, no," said Colm.

"He wants out then?" asked Vasarely. "Figured I'd shoot him on sight, maybe."

"Maybe," said Colm.

"Might be easier," said Vasarely, leaning back in his chair.

"There's not many partisans left, but enough to cause trouble. He just wants out."

Vasarely nodded, throwing out a less than reasonable number for everything Grimmley had left.

"It's that or a walk off the pier," said Vasarely.

Colm nodded.

"You got that in the war?" asked Vasarely, motioning to the walking stick.

Colm nodded.

"The limp, not the stick."

"You're Steiner. You've been in a bloody mess or two. What was that nonsense in Guyana?"

"I'd call it unfortunate and leave it at that."

"You're still with that enquiry outfit?"

"I'm on hiatus."

"Would that preclude you from taking on other opportunities?"

"Such as?"

"There's a small city on the coast where we send the liquor. I own a few pubs and dance halls there, some other businesses. One of our ships went missing. My men there don't know what happened apparently. I still require their services to ensure the delivery of the product, and these are relationships that go way back. I'd prefer to know something definite before I torch the city. And it'd be better if it was an outsider undoing the knots."

"I'll figure out what's happening."

"Good man," said Vasarely.

PART X

Colm took a train to Glasgow a few days later, and then another to Vasarely's coastal fiefdom. It deposited him by daylight in a run-down portion of the small city, filled with black brick tenements and smoke-stacked factories aching darkness into the sky above the ocean. Colm got a room at a gray-brick hotel near the station, depositing his belongings on a sooty bed in a tiny room that loomed over rows of buildings which rolled down the surf into the water.

Colm thumbed through a hand-written list of Vasarely's properties, comparing it against the map of the city he'd gotten at the train station. That night, he found the off-books pub near the docks, a rough-looking wooden building with boarded up windows. A portly doorman in a long coat let him through a side door, and Colm entered the bleak, sconce-lit establishment. He posted himself against the back wall with a few drinks and watched fishermen and factory workers in drab clothing sullenly nurse booze.

Colm approached the barkeep, a thin man with long scraggly hair.

"Suppose I were interested in the races. Who would I

speak with?"

"McTavish," the barkeep said, gesturing to a table of men against the other wall, seemingly led by a blonde-haired youth in a smart blue suit. Colm walked over to them.

"You're taking bets?" asked Colm.

"From people I know," said McTavish.

"Then why don't we get to know each other. I'll buy a round for the table."

McTavish looked Colm over.

"Fuck off," he said.

Colm walked over to the bartender and bought another drink.

"Didn't take," said Colm.

"That's how it is all over these days," said the barkeep.

"Who does he work for?"

"Supposed to be one of Trocadero's people."

"They have some kind of a dispute?"

"Maybe. It's chaos these days. Half the men are in France, the ones that come back are blown to hell. So if you have some kind of vice, this is what you're dealing with."

"You hear anything about a ship that went missing?"

The barkeep laughed.

"That's not a mystery. That's what I mean. Everyone knows what happened to the ship."

"Boss back in London doesn't know."

"He doesn't know a lot of things. Doesn't know there's no one here to trust anymore. Little fuckers burned it down. Got drunk, burned it down."

"McTavish?" Colm gestured over his shoulder.

"No, but he had a good laugh about it with the ones that did. They came in here, smelling of pitch and liquor afterwards. Probably went to every pub in the city that night. Ruffian named Herbert and a few of his friends. Squiggles and Pickpocket I think they were called."

"Where would they be tonight?"

"There's another one of these a few streets away."

Colm consulted his list and rattled an address off to the barkeep.

"Yeah, that's the one."

Colm paid the barkeep a few extra shillings, then walked over to the next pub. It was a similarly rickety wooden building, though it had no porter. Inside, half the tables were filled with smoking ruffians and prostitutes. There was a fight in progress on the far side of the bar, where the bartender, a brown-haired woman in a white dress, was attempting to keep the peace. When she ventured over to Colm's spot at the counter, he bought two gins. He downed one, then waved his hand to get her attention.

"I'm looking for Herbert or Trocadero," he told the woman.

"Trocadero is in the center, Herbert's to his left." She pointed to a table against the back wall, where three men in gray suits and hats lounged and smoked beside opium-dazed women in loose dark dresses. Trocadero was lithe, with a thin mustache. Herbert was stockier, with a stubble of blonde hair.

"Give me a bottle of whatever they're drinking," said Colm, dropping money on the counter. She handed him a bottle of whiskey, and he walked over to them, placing it on the table.

"I do you some kind of favor?" asked Trocadero.

"Not yet," said Colm. "I need some strong arms for a bad deed."

"We might know somebody," said Trocadero.

"There's men in Glasgow that need to be dealt with," Colm said. "Warehouse near the docks. A torch job."

"Something we could handle," said Herbert.

"I need it laid to waste. Everything this fucker ever touched," said Colm, barely containing a seething rage as he drank his gin. "I want to watch it burn."

"Nothing like it," said Herbert. "Pretty too, the flames

and the smolder against the waves."

"Never seen it before," said Colm.

"Did one about two months ago," Herbert said.

"Yeah?"

"Owned by this fucker who thinks he still runs this town. Vasarely."

"Easy," said Trocadero.

"But he doesn't," said Herbert. "No matter who he sends to make trouble."

Colm gripped the pistol in his coat and aimed it underneath the table.

"You make a fast move, there's gonna be a faster one through the back of your skull," said Trocadero as Colm felt a gun barrel graze his head.

"And I put one through your gut," said Colm.

Herbert glanced under the table, confirming Colm's weapon.

"Yeah, he's got one on you," Herbert laughed. Trocadero did not look amused.

"I'm a messenger," said Colm. "It's up to you whether you'll be in a state to receive messages in the future. Be fucking civilized."

Colm felt the barrel slide away from his head. He slipped the gun into his coat pocket as he stood, but kept it aimed at Trocadero. He walked past the fourth man, and through the door.

As he got to the end of the street, two gunshots hit the pavement near him. He spun and fired twice at the club, striking one of the four men pursuing him. He continued walking towards the hotel, and more gunshots rang out after him. He hid behind a car and fired twice, then stumbled into an alley between buildings. From there, he crossed over to the next street.

As Colm emerged from the darkness, two of Trocadero's men appeared on his right from another alley. All three men fired. One of his pursuers dropped dead, and the other got lucky with a shot that struck Colm's torso. Colm slunk against the wall, firing twice more, the second shot striking the other assailant in the neck. The man dropped to the ground and gurgled a death rattle.

Colm touched his stomach, and found he was bleeding badly.

He stood and limped towards the hotel.

Inside his room, he quickly bandaged the wound, grabbed his haversack and set off again. Trawling the streets, he spied an older Model T tucked away in a property behind a single-story, white wooden house. He grabbed a handful of cash, stuffed it in their mailbox, then started the car and drove down the road leading to Glasgow.

He abandoned the car in a patch of woods outside of the city, then found a cheap motel in the East End. He used their telephone to contact Vasarely the next morning, explaining the mess to the best of his ability.

"A valuable reappraisal," Vasarely concluded.

After they were done speaking, Colm checked his wound. It ached but had stopped bleeding. He changed the bandages, then walked to the station and purchased a train ticket to London. By the time he got there, Vasarely had set his agents loose in the port city, and there was already a story in the newspaper about a string of arsons.

Colm had himself stitched up at a doctor's office near Hereford, then took a cab to Vasarely's pub. Inside the back room, Vasarely slid Colm an envelope stuffed with cash.

"Trocadero and Herbert?" Colm asked.

"Piles of dust," said Vasarely.

"Beat us to it," said Colm, tapping the envelope on the desk before he left. He took another cab back to his flat in Hereford. When he got there, he made himself a cup of tea, read the newspaper, then went to bed.

Upon waking the next morning, he found there was a typed note from Clotilde slid under the door, telling him to return to the office the following week for a briefing on his next case.

PART XI

It was another gray day when Colm finally went back to the enquiry service, but his spirits were buoyed by the impending return to normalcy. However, a short distance from the building, he felt something was off. He placed his hand on his pistol and swung the unlocked door open.

Clotilde was lying face down on her desk. Both of the other doors inside the room were open. Colm drew his pistol, then closed the entrance behind him. He walked over to Clotilde and checked her nonexistent pulse. There were two bloody blooms on her white blouse from the assassin's bullets. Colm went into the archive behind her, briefly looking at the two rows of overturned steel filing cabinets in the blue room before returning to the office.

He walked through the other opening, creeping up the steps to the floor above. When he got there, it was completely empty. No desks, no papers, no sign of the Men Upstairs. Colm took a final tender look at Clotilde before he hurried out the door towards the White Feather.

When Colm arrived, there were dark shades thrown across the windows and no lights visible within. He tried the door, but it was locked. He looked around, concerned about encroaching patrols, but pulled out his picks anyway and undid the lock. Then he drew his pistol and stepped inside.

The room was empty and dark, except for crevices of light from broken boards in the walls. Colm could hear talking in the storage room in back, punctuated by short howls of pain. He walked slowly towards the room, then heard a creak of boards as someone walked to its door and opened it.

It was one of Vasarely's men in a trench coat. Colm shot him in the stomach twice, and he dropped to the ground, screaming. Within the room was a scuffle of movement. Colm fired at the blur and heard another cry of agony. Colm walked over to the fallen man in front of him, shot him through both hands, then continued into the room.

Grimmley was tied to a chair between casks of wine. He was bleeding from his torso and his face was misshapen from the beating. The other assassin was crawling on the floor towards his gun. Colm shot him through the neck. As he gurgled, Colm undid Grimmley's knots. When the ropes came undone, Grimmley's intestines spilled out.

"I'm not sure they can stitch that up," Grimmley remarked.

"They stormed the enquiry office," Colm said. "Clotilde's dead. It would appear Vasarely's assurances of a clean break were exaggerated."

Colm walked over to the man with the wounded hands howling in pain and lifted him by his hair.

"Trocadero sent you?" Colm asked.

"Trocadero's dead," said the assassin.

"Then explain why you're here," Colm said.

"Vasarely needed to clean house, but he couldn't get rid of all the bad apples in Scotland. He had to make a deal with who was left to keep the ships moving. Blamed you and Grimmley for the arsons and executions. Promised them your heads as a show of good faith."

"He's still holed up at that gaudy pub?" asked Colm.

The man didn't answer, just stared with rage as he expired. His companion had died at some point in the conversation. It was just Colm and Grimmley left. Colm walked into the bar and came back with a bottle of whiskey. He helped Grimmley take a swig, then took one himself. Colm gripped his friend's shoulder as he nodded off into nothingness. Colm took the dead men's pistols and placed them in his coat.

Then he went to the bar and lined up four bottles of vodka on the counter. He tore down one of the curtains, cut fuses from them, and stuffed them into the bottles. He found a box of matches from behind the counter and placed it in his coat. He grabbed a leather satchel from the storage room and placed the bottles inside it.

Colm re-loaded his pistol and placed it in his right pocket. Then he slung the satchel over his shoulder, exiting the Wild Feather and beginning the walk to Vasarely's pub.

Two of Vasarely's men were standing outside the club as he approached. He drew his pistol and shot them both in the chest. He put the satchel down, grabbed a bottle from it, lit the fuse, and tossed it through the window of the pub. It exploded within as the pub's patrons howled in surprise.

He lit another one and tossed it through another window. It smashed across the floor. Flames and smoke twisted inside. Another of Vasarely's men broke one of the glass panes and fired at Colm. One of the shots struck a car nearby, the other struck his bad arm. Colm fired twice at the window and the shooter disappeared.

The crowd streamed through the back entrance into the road beyond. Colm slung the satchel over himself and walked to the front door. When he shouldered it open, another bullet struck the wall close to his head. He spun towards the assailant, firing twice and dropping the suited man. Vasarely and one of his underlings emerged from the back room with pistols and shot at Colm. He fired his last two bullets, and they ducked behind the wall in the office.

Colm grabbed another of the incendiaries and lit it. As he tossed it, Vasarely fired again, the round striking Colm's stomach. The bomb only half-cleared the floor, setting a table between them on fire. Colm sunk to his knees and took a spare gun from his pocket but couldn't lift it all the way. He laid down flat on his side and aimed at the men's knees through the smoke and flames.

He shot out the underling's left leg and when the man toppled over, he placed another bullet in his head. As Vasarely ran for the back door, Colm fired a round into his back and he fell forward. The blaze was overtaking the entire room, smoke clouded everything. Colm crawled along the floor until he made it to Vasarely, who was attempting to right himself with a barstool.

Colm lifted the gun as high as he could and plugged Vasarely twice in the back. Vasarely fell to the ground, heaved a set of rapid breaths and then stopped moving. Colm grabbed onto the counter and lifted himself to his feet. He snatched the satchel, then limped through the front entrance. He stumbled into an alley and took a series of back roads to Hereford Street. He used the side passage up the staircase, and crashed along the landing, slamming the door shut behind him.

He left the lights out.

The sky ached red beyond the window.

He removed the last bottle of booze from the satchel and sat down on the sofa. He poured half the bottle on his wounds and drank the rest. He laid his head down, unsure if he would bleed out or be captured. It mattered less to him than the dying sunset that dulled his senses as the abattoir awakened below.

PART XII

Colm woke coughing blood. He had, to his displeasure, survived the night. The doctor's office he'd used in previous weeks catered to some of Vasarely's men so he couldn't count on their discretion. He cleaned his wounds in the sink then took a seat at the table where he made artless stitches with his trembling hand. Then he dug through the cabinet and finished off another bottle of gin.

Staring out his window, he began considering Vasarely's network of accomplices, and thought it best to leave the city for at least a while. There was a monastery on the coast he'd visited a few years back where he'd made the acquaintance of an abbot named McDougall. He changed into a clean hazel suit, packed his essentials into a haversack, then made for the train station. He dozed the four-hour journey beside a crocheting woman in white who woke him to disembark.

He stumbled off the platform and found a coachman willing to make the last leg of the journey. They passed through a small village at the foot of the monastery, which was filled with a few rows of shops and houses past the main road. The coach deposited him at the low stone curtain on the outskirts of the monastery. Colm paid his fare and the man left.

The monastery was comprised of a stone chapel and a cluster of a half dozen buildings, beyond which lay a field of barley crops descending the opposite slope of the hill. McDougall, a tough old man with a bushy head of white hair and a matching beard, wore a dark blue robe rolled up to his elbows. He labored with a scythe, slashing the ripened barley into piles along the incline. Lower down the hill, two other monks in matching robes performed the same task.

Colm waved weakly to McDougall, who motioned his companions over. The three men escorted Colm to the dormitory. Within were two rows of stone cells, most lacking signs of occupation as the men stepped past them. They led Colm into one of the little rooms and laid him down on a bed. One of McDougall's companions, a thin, bald monk with spectacles, undid Colm's bandages and shook his head.

"I'm Brother Matteo. I'll need to redo these," he said.

"I'd be much obliged," said Colm.

"This is Brother Malvolio," McDougall said, gesturing to the shorter, thicker monk with brown hair.

"I'm Colm Steiner, it's a pleasure," he said.

Brother Matteo finished stitching the wounds and put on clean bandages. Colm waited for the men to leave, then took a few swigs of gin from the bottle in his haversack before he passed out.

McDougall knocked at the cell door a few hours later, entering with a plate of vegetables and meat.

"I appreciate this very much," said Colm, mouthing down the food.

"Is it wise to ask what led to the maiming?"

"That business is done," said Colm. "How have you been?"

"We've been blessed with a relative calm," said McDougall. "We're kept busy with the fields, holding services for the townsfolk. Attending to women deprived of their kin."

"Rough all around," said Colm.

McDougall nodded.

"Matteo will be in to check the bandages tomorrow."

McDougall left. Colm finished the platter, then laid his head back and fell asleep.

In the morning, Matteo returned and changed the bandages. Afterwards, Colm watched the men work in the field outside his window. McDougall came back that afternoon to share the midday meal with Colm. They spoke little, but warmly. When they were finished eating, McDougall left Colm a few novels from the library and went back to his duties. Colm spent the day reading. He saw Matteo again that evening before he fell asleep.

A few days into his convalescence, Colm was feeling well enough to go for walks. He circled the grounds with a borrowed cane from McDougall, having misplaced his at some point in the London fracas. Within the cluster of buildings was a flower garden he quite enjoyed, spending an hour or so reading there after the midday meal. While he was there was one afternoon, he heard a commotion down the hillside. He walked over to investigate and saw a dark-haired woman in riding gear leading a roan over to McDougall.

The horse was whinnying and frantically shying away from the conversation, and the woman seemed to be apologizing to the monk. After another few exchanges, she led the horse back along the road to town.

Colm took his evening meal with the monks in the refectory. They sat at one of two wooden tables perpendicular to the dais, situated along the candle-sconced stone walls. Colm asked McDougall about the woman.

"Her name's Orsinia, she runs the livery in the village. I was supposed to go into town a few days ago to see about a new horse but it slipped my mind entirely."

"She runs the livery by herself?" Colm asked.

"Her brother and father are still in France."

"What was the matter with the horse?"

"She said he's been skittish since last night. She heard him cry out in the darkness, and went to the stable to check on him, but she didn't find anything. She's been by his side since then, trying to calm him down."

"Have there been other robberies lately?"

McDougall shook his head.

"The war's hollowed the town out. But wars don't last forever."

After the meal was finished, the men retired to the cells for bed.

Sometime in the night, Colm heard the woman's screams.

Colm walked into the hallway of the dormitory at the same moment as Matteo and Malvolio.

"Where's McDougall?" Colm asked.

"He's often in the library this time of night," said Matteo as the three men moved toward the noise.

Orsinia held a candle in front of her as she ambled up the hillside in a loose white night dress. When she got near, Colm could see she was covered in blood. Matteo ran over to her, but she shook her head as he inspected her.

"No, it's...they've killed my horses."

McDougall, lantern in hand, finally made his way over from the library, and Orsinia repeated her situation.

"We'll need to go down there," said McDougall.

"You and I," said Colm. "She should stay with Matteo and Malvolio."

McDougall nodded, then he and Colm walked down the hill, turning left at the first building on the main road. The livery was on the edge of town, adjoined to Orsinia's thatched-roof cottage. The cottage was dimly lit, the livery was completely dark.

Colm drew his pistol and walked ahead of McDougall into the open wooden doors of the stable. There was no noise within. The lantern light threw slivers of yellow against the two rows of stalls. They looked into the first one, and within, a horse was lying bloodied and lifeless.

Colm and McDougall did a cursory scan of the rest, finding the same sight in each stall. They walked into Orsinia's cottage, a simple wooden living room and kitchen joined to two bedrooms by a hallway. They found nothing to indicate it had been breached as part of the attack.

"Is there a constable on duty?"

"Next town over, four miles down the road. We can telephone him in the morning. Not sure what good another body stumbling around in the dark would do."

"Oughta cover 'em at least until we can get back," said Colm.

"All right," agreed McDougall. Behind the property was a vacant corral and a tool shed where they found canvas sheets, which they draped across the bodies. They walked back up the hill to the monastery. The other monks had made another room up for Orsinia. McDougall checked to see if she had revealed any new information, but they said she hadn't. In the morning, McDougall called the constable, but he was dealing with a murder all day and didn't think he'd be able to make it until the following morning.

The monks left Colm to look after Orsinia, then travelled back to the livery to bury the bodies. He went to his room and read until he heard her stirring. He greeted her wordlessly in the hallway. The two of them walked to the refectory, where they shared tea and meat Malvolio had left for them.

"No one else had been by in the previous weeks?" he asked.

"People pass through. I can't..."

She drank the rest of her tea solemnly.

The monks arrived a few hours later and escorted her back to the cottage.

When they returned from that final errand and began

their daily routine, Colm took a longer walk into town. He stopped in a few shops along the main road, rarely staying in any for more than a few moments. Finally, he pursued his true aim and went to the stable to look for clues in daylight. He could see now where the intruder had forced the door's lock by the scrapes on the wooden exterior, but inside, there was little beyond the upsetting sight of bloodstains that lingered on the floorboards. He walked into the area behind the property, where the vacant corrals and quiet storage sheds were still haunted in the sunlight. The dirt atop the horses' mass grave was visible where the estate met the treeline. The road out of town continued to the left of the property.

In the house, he could hear Orsinia sobbing.

Colm ventured to the edge of the forest and searched for signs of habitation. He found a burned out cook fire there, no longer warm. The footprints around the fire were curious. The owner's right boot seemed to be missing a bottom section, because occasionally the outer toes would appear in the dirt.

Colm returned to the monastery.

The evening was tense, but without incident. The next morning, Colm took another walk into town. He stopped in the small wooden grocery store, run by a frail, elderly woman in a brown dress named Bellaria. He asked if she noticed any strange men around. She mentioned a white-haired man in a ratty black coat who had requested anything she was tossing out.

"He's been in here before?"

"Once last week I believe. Wearing the same coat."

"No idea where he might be staying?"

She shook her head.

Colm returned to the monastery. After supper, he went for a late-night stroll through the grounds. As he made it to the edge of the barley fields, he saw a small campfire in the distant woods, and began walking towards it. Seated around the campfire was an old man with white hair and a ratty black coat singing a sea shanty. He stared at Colm with wild eyes, cooking a slab of meat over the fire with a stick.

"Would you like some?" he asked Colm, gesturing with the stick.

"What is it?"

"Chicken, maybe. Maybe not."

Colm looked at the man's tattered boots, noticing the hole in the right one.

"What's your name?"

"Windsor."

"I'm Colm. How long have you been here?"

"Just a few days," he said. "Then it's off again, somewhere."

"Your boots have seen better days."

"They have. I should find another pair soon."

"You were staying closer to town a few nights ago."

"Maybe. Hard to tell in the dark."

"Were you near the livery?"

"I didn't see anything," Windsor said.

"Did you hear anything?"

Windsor winced at his own recollection.

Colm walked closer to the man. He didn't see any blood on him, though he supposed he might have switched into another set of clothing after the crime.

"Something bad happened," Windsor said. "Could hear something bad happening. Walked over, and they were already..."

"You saw something then," said Colm.

"There was a man there, maybe."

"Tell me about him."

"Looked like the lass a bit. Relation, I suspect."

Colm nodded.

"Will you be around for a while? I could wrangle you something from the shop in the morning."

"Oughta be," said Windsor.

Colm walked to the refectory, where he found

McDougall studying an illustrated manuscript. He told him what he'd heard from Windsor.

"Her brother Ferdinand might be back."

"Were there troubles with him before?" Colm asked.

"He was a rough sort. Quite protective of the girl. It bordered on something salacious. The old man took special pains to escort him to France."

Colm went to bed. When he woke the next morning, he went to the market to make good on his promise. After purchasing a bag of groceries, he returned to the campfire in the woods. When he arrived, the fire was dead, and there were bloodstains soaked into the ground beside it. Colm searched the nearby forest but couldn't find Windsor's body anywhere.

He walked back to Orsinia's cottage and knocked on the door. She answered, wearing a loose tan blouse and black pants. She invited him inside the small kitchen for a cup of tea.

"Has your brother been in contact with you?"

"Why would you ask about him?"

Colm shrugged his shoulders.

"He'd sent a telegram some time back, saying he'd be returning. An injury."

"He never arrived?"

"You suspect him?"

"Someone might have seen him around."

"Who?"

"A man I am unable to locate."

"There you have it, a man covering his own tracks. Who sent you on a wild goose chase that gave him time to escape."

"Maybe," said Colm. "I have been deceived before. Should your brother return, I might urge caution. Thank you for the tea."

Colm went back to the monastery. His wounds were almost healed, but he couldn't return to London. He had wanted to see Canada for some time and thought it might be a good spot to lay low for a few years. He told his plans to McDougall that evening as the brothers were gathering barley into wicker baskets in the field.

"Suppose it's better than whatever trouble you'd run into back north. Kin that way?"

"No," said Colm.

"Shame. Something charming about reunions. I just saw Orsinia and Ferdinand conspiring in the streets. Brought to mind some of their youthful adventures."

"The father was nowhere to be seen?"

"Killed at the Somme, apparently," said McDougall.

"Will you be keeping a watchful eye?"

"You haven't seen the Windsor fella?"

"I have not."

"Then it's an open case, in my estimation."

Colm was nearly ready to begin his journey across the ocean. However, he retained some curiosity about the siblings, as well as a fear the violence might spill over into the monastery. He made a final trip down to Orsinia's property one afternoon. He knocked on the door, but there wasn't any answer. As he was about to leave, the dark-haired Ferdinand emerged from the stable in a dirty white shirt and riding pants. He did look nearly the spitting image of Orsinia.

"Some business this way?"

"Just thought I'd check in on your sister."

"Friend of hers."

"We're not so close. I just met her through an acquaintance."

"The monk."

Colm nodded. Ferdinand looked at Colm's cane.

"You get that in France?"

"The limp, not the cane. I'm sorry to hear your father didn't make it. And what happened to the horses was an atrocity. Do you plan on buying more?"

"They belonged to the old man. I didn't share his affection for the creatures."

"Orsinia seemed quite fond of them," said Colm.

"Yes. The incident was unfortunate."

"If you'd give her my good tidings, I'd be grateful," said Colm.

Ferdinand nodded. Colm left.

When it got dark, he returned to the property. The door to the livery was still open. He walked inside and looked into the stalls, but nothing had changed since his last visit. There was movement within the house. He crept around the perimeter and heard a shuffling of footsteps. Beside the back door was a pile of logs. Colm grabbed a few, walked over to the vacant corral and started a small fire inside the wooden gate. Then he grabbed a few pebbles from the dirt, walked to the back of the house and tossed them at the window before scurrying to a hiding spot in the livery.

Ferdinand opened the back door holding a rifle and cautiously walked over to the fire. Colm ran inside the house. It reeked. There was no sign of Orsinia in the kitchen or living room. He went to the bedroom door, which was locked. He knocked on it lightly, but there was no answer within. He forced the door.

Orsinia was tied up on the bed in a loose white shift. She had been dead for days. The floorboards creaked on the other side of the wall. Colm drew his pistol and fired twice through the wood. Something slumped against the floor. He crept to the frame and peeked around the edge. Ferdinand was dead.

Colm snuck back into the monastery, grabbed his haversack, then started on the road to the nearest port.

PART XIII

Colm purchased passage on a steamer headed to Quebec. He had a private room for the voyage, and rarely ventured out into the communal areas. On the second morning of the trip, he was in the dining facility for a meal, when a gentleman with short gray hair and a black suit walked in with a black satchel. He filled a plate and sat down at the table beside Colm's.

Halfway through the meal, the man turned to Colm and spoke.

"How are you enjoying the trip?" the man asked.

"The lack of disaster thus far has endeared it to me," said Colm.

The man faked a smile.

"Quite humorous," he said. "My name is Francoise Leger. And yours?"

"Colm Steiner."

"You're testing your fortunes in the New World?"

"Might as well, I figured. I've already tested them to their limits elsewhere."

"It's a place of grand possibilities. Though I often find myself splitting the year between England and Quebec. Family, you see."

"Wife and children?" Colm asked politely.

"The wife was sadly claimed by God, though I am blessed with two young children, currently back in the Commonwealth with relatives."

"It must be an agony to part with them."

"Aye."

"Then why do it?"

"Alas, my business interests overseas require a heavy hand best delivered in person."

"What's your business?" asked Colm.

"I operate a series of drug stores throughout Quebec. I'm something of a physician, myself."

"Is that right?"

"Not strictly licensed, you understand?"

"I'm beginning to."

"It's not like that. It's mostly above board."

"I'm curious about what isn't."

"I dabble in more experimental methods."

Leger motioned to his satchel.

"I noticed you have a limp."

"Quite observant."

"It ails you?"

"Less than it did before."

"Suppose I might ease your troubles further."

Colm looked at the satchel. Leger placed it on the table and removed a metal rod from it.

"Mesmerism," said Colm.

"Some charlatans have tainted the word for you. Speak your mind."

"Men must make their way in the world, this I understand. But I'd prefer not to share my table with snake oil salesmen. Should I see you plying your wares in my presence, this conversation will be reiterated most unpleasantly."

Leger packed up his satchel, grabbed his plate and left the dining hall. Colm finished his meal and returned to his room. The next few days proceeded without incident. The day before the ship was to reach the mainland, there was a commotion in the hall outside his door. Colm stepped outside and saw an elderly couple in a matching dark suit and dress arguing two doors away. The woman stepped into the room and slammed the door and the man started walking solemnly to the stairs leading to the deck. Colm went back into his room but got a hankering for a cigarette and ventured up the same way a short time later.

The old man was leaned against the ship's rail smoking a cigarette. Colm stood next to him.

"Troubles with the missus?"

"Now and forever," he said. "Told off a lunatic who tried to sell us some nonsense earlier. She was gabbing with him anyway just to run my temperature up, I suppose. After a certain number of years, it gets to be a war of attrition."

"What would winning look like?"

"Exactly," said the old man. "Simply a state of affairs. What's good outweighs what isn't every moment of the day."

"When you stop to think about it," says Colm.

"Which I guess is the key," said the old man. "Reminding myself how ugly things might really get. Pettiness blinds beauty. Arrogance flecks mud in the eye of grace. It's an affront."

"Aye," said Colm. They finished their cigarettes in silence. Colm walked back to his cabin.

PART XIV

Colm found a flat in Montreal much like the one he'd had in London. It had a bedroom and a kitchen connected to a living room, with roughly the same furniture set-up, though the walls were decorated in dark green. After a few weeks of getting used to the city, he ventured over to an enquiry service he'd dealt with briefly in the past, managed by a British expat named Rudolph Beringar.

The three-story office was nestled along a surprisingly busy side-street, its front partially hidden by an oak tree. The enquiry office comprised only the first floor of the building, the other two were apparently being used by the local government. Colm knocked and was let inside by a young, blonde-haired secretary in a red skirt-suit named Edith. The walls were bead-boarded, and the carpets were a dark red that complemented Edith's outfit. She led Colm past her desk through another door into a hallway that branched off three times. The first two doors were marked as archives, the final door had a sign that read 'office.'

Edith knocked twice.

"Come in," Beringar said from inside. His office possessed a walnut desk, filing cabinets to its right, and a window to a small garden courtyard between buildings.

Beringar was a thin man with reddish-brown hair and a prominent nose, wearing a brown suit and polished brown shoes.

He stood and shook Colm's hand, and the two men took a seat as Edith left.

"That was some ugliness back in London."

"I sorted it out as best I could," said Colm.

"In certain ways, it's less messy here. The things our company deals with anyway. The Men Upstairs spoke highly of you. I just wanted to meet you."

"To make sure they'd glued me back together properly."

"It was a concern," said Beringar. "You'll be dealing with Edith mostly, but I wanted to give you this first case myself. It's a bit of a soft throw, but it needs doing."

Beringar slid a dark red envelope across the table. Colm opened it and leafed through the typed documents within. Attached to them was a picture of a woman with short dark hair and large eyes.

"Missing persons case. University student named Dorothy Fitzclarence. Disappeared a few weeks back. Parents are in England. Flatmate says she went out for a pint with a colleague and never returned."

"Colleague's name?"

"Unknown. Dorothy's address is below."

Colm left the office and found the girl's apartment. The other woman living there was a redhead named Sylvia. She wore a floral dress and dusted the crevices of the living room's white walls while Colm sat at a table in front of a stack of newspapers.

"Don't know anything about the bloke."

"Were there any places nearby she liked going?"

"Pub called the Bleeding Anchor down the road. Folks from class go there."

"Are you expecting company?"

"I'm showing some people her room. Just in case you don't find her."

"Can I see it?"

Sylvia led him into one of the two bedrooms off the hallway. There was a bed, an armoire, a cabinet and a bookshelf inside. Colm rifled through the cabinet and armoire first, finding only magazines and clothing. Then he looked in the bookshelf and dug out a leather address book that listed some of her contacts from school. He thanked Sylvia, then left.

His first stop was the Bleeding Anchor. Blue lights buzzed above the bar, where a rotund man in coveralls named Clyde poured another pint for his only customer, an older gentleman in a sweater vest reading a newspaper at the far end of the counter.

Colm showed Clyde the girl's photograph.

"I think so. By herself a while over at the table near the door. Fella came in an hour later."

"What'd he look like?"

"Another student maybe. Slicked back hair. Sharp jaw. Dress shirt with the sleeves rolled up, and black pants. Ordered them a round of pints, then they fucked off somewhere."

"You'd recognize him if he came back?"

"I would."

"I'll check back."

Colm went to his flat, took a seat in the kitchen and began dialing the contacts from Dorothy's leather address book. The first two women only knew her in passing, but the third, Patricia, sounded crestfallen. She agreed to meet him in a cafe down the road from her apartment.

She was seated at a table near the back of the darkened wooden room when Colm entered. She had crimped blonde hair and wore a white blouse and matching skirt.

"You spoke to her the day she disappeared?"

Patricia nodded.

"She mention meeting someone?"

Patricia sipped coffee from a gray mug, working her way up to the answer.

"She'd gotten pregnant. Needed to get it fixed. Found a man who could help her."

"Through another girl from class?"

"Yeah, girl had it done last year. Gave Dorothy the number."

"You had her write it down for you, just in case?"

Patricia nodded sheepishly.

"The boys aren't careful. Even when you ask them to be."

She slid a slip of paper across the table.

"I might need your help again, Patricia."

"Just call me," she said, and left.

Colm went back to his apartment, smoked a cigarette, and dialed the number. A man with a deep voice answered.

"Hello?" said the voice.

"I know a girl in trouble."

"They make 'em that way, mate."

"Heard you had methods to mend them."

"Methods, yes. Methods for money."

"I'd like to meet you first. This girl is quite important to me."

"Fine."

"I'm near the Bleeding Anchor, have you heard of it?"

"No, I'm across town."

He gave the name of another pub and told Colm to meet him there in a few hours. It was about a mile from Colm's apartment, and he got there early. This one was dimly lit yellow and purple within. The bartender, a tiny bald man in a white shirt, chatted with two middle-aged women in floppy hats and white dresses sitting across from him. Colm ordered a gin and sat down at one of the tables off to the left side of the room.

A short time later, the man with the sharp jaw and slicked back hair and a blue dress shirt rolled up to his elbows entered the establishment. He smoked his cigarette with swagger and sat down across from Colm. He slid a paper across the table with the cost of the procedure.

"Non-negotiable."

"Fine," Colm said.

"You married or something? Knock some floozy up?"

"When can you do it?"

"Day after next."

"Where?"

"Money up front, details after."

Colm pulled cash from his jacket and slid it across the table.

The man with the sharp jaw pocketed the cash, then took another piece of paper from his pocket and slid that across the table.

"That's the address. 8 a.m. She'll be no good the rest of the day."

The man with the sharp jaw stood up and left.

Two days later, Colm went to the address, which was part of a small complex of three and four-story brick buildings near the docks along the Ottawa River. He suspected it was a trap and kept his right hand on his pocketed M1911.

He knocked on the building's metal door. The man with the sharp jaw opened it, and Colm drew his pistol.

"Walk inside," said Colm.

The man led him along an uncarpeted concrete hallway. The walls were particle board and there was only one inlet, a dark space on the left. The man with the sharp jaw led Colm to the entryway. Concrete stairs led to darkness below. There was a blue light shining from a corner of the black room.

"Are they here?" a whispery voice called from below. The sharp-jawed man looked at Colm to see if he should answer. Colm shook his head then pointed down the steps. They walked down carefully. At the far end of the room, there was a large bald man in a doctor's coat standing in between a medical table and a shelf filled with surgical instruments.

"There was a girl here a few weeks ago named

Dorothy," Colm said.

"They give fake names sometimes," said the man in the doctor's coat.

"This one didn't."

"That's right," said the man in the doctor's coat.

"How do you get rid of the babies when you're done?"

"Incinerator," said the man in the doctor's coat.

"So I suppose there's no use in looking for the girl's body."

The man in the doctor's coat didn't say anything, but his eyes flashed a wicked confession. Colm slammed his pistol against the sharp-jawed man's skull. He fell and attempted to lift himself and Colm struck him twice more against the back of the head.

"Turn around," Colm said, walking over to the man in the doctor's coat. "I won't hurt..."

The man grabbed a surgical knife from the shelf, and Colm shot him in the stomach. The man slumped to his knees and stared at the gushing wound. Colm tied both of the men up with rope, found a telephone and dialed the local constable. When the police arrived, he described the situation to the best of his ability. Afterwards, he ventured home, dialed in a report to Edith and then went to bed.

PART XV

It was a warm, bright day in Montreal when Colm returned to the enquiry office. According to Edith, a local art dealer named Vic Stebbins had gone missing. Stebbins' partner, a Mr. Van der Vecken, had approached the office with the case, but was afraid to go to local authorities because of a recent deal with unsavory characters. Colm found Stebbins' contact information in his dark red envelope and ventured to the art gallery, which was situated along a busy main road of the city.

Colm peered through the black building's glass facade. The walls were a bright yellow, the main room displayed a few paintings by local unknowns in the style of Hoger and Klimt. Men were seated at a circle of chairs within, where they watched a long-haired, blonde youngster in a tattered gray coat speak passionately as he read from a pamphlet. The men clapped at the end of the meeting and filed out of the building.

Colm walked inside as the youngster began placing the chairs in a neat pile near a door in the back of the room.

"They seemed enthralled. What was the topic?" asked Colm.

"The changing times," said the youngster, handing

Colm a pamphlet on dismantling the machinery of capitalism.

"In the style of the Russians, then?"

"It's sweeping the world, comrade," said the youngster. "We meet again here next week, your presence would be most welcome."

"I'd call that a misguided assumption at best," said Colm, handing back the pamphlet. "Fear not, I've gleaned the necessary elements from the document there."

"I wish you well, anyway," said the youngster, leaving the art studio.

Colm walked to the back room and knocked on the door.

"I'm from the enquiry service."

The door opened. A man with curly hair and a black shirt and pants opened the door, smoking a cigarette. Behind him were rows of crates leading up to a back door, with a few paintings placed carelessly atop the boxes.

"When is the last time you saw him?"

"Two weeks back," said Van der Vecken. "He was fond of last-minute adventures with women who didn't know better than to trust him. I figured I'd receive a phone call from Europe at some point."

"And why are you certain you won't?"

Van der Vecken walked over to one of the crates and pulled out an envelope which he handed to Colm, who read it aloud:

"'Return the Kubin.' This is Alfred Kubin?" Colm asked. Van der Vecken nodded.

"We bought it as part of an estate sale, clear chain of custody. The kidnapper has no claim on the property."

"Beyond a knife at your friend's throat, presumably. Where was the location of this estate sale?"

"A manor beyond the city limits. Completely abandoned."

"You'd like me to return with both the painting and your friend?"

"The ransomers won't have both at any rate, I've had a local mock up a copy. The orator you may have met in the gallery. Wilhelm."

Van der Vecken walked over to a painting wrapped in brown paper, hidden between two crates. He handed it to Colm. There was a scrap of paper attached to it with the address.

"Tomorrow at noon. Please report back as soon as it's through."

Colm took the painting and returned to his apartment. It was a good distance outside the city, and since there was a possibility of unpleasantness, he requisitioned the company's Model T for the trip instead of using a coach.

After a rough drive over dirt roads, the decrepit gray manor opened up on a piece of flat grassland between patches of trees. Colm parked near the house, slung the satchel with the painting over his shoulder, and kept his right hand on his pocketed pistol as he approached the building.

He pushed the open door wide. The floor was checker-patterned, sunlight pierced glass above the circular staircase twisting in front of him. In the center of the room were two men in dark coats and face masks holding pistols. In between them was another man with a sack over his head, tied to a chair.

Colm lowered the satchel to the ground and stepped back. One of the men walked over to it, picked it up and inspected the painting within. He nodded. The other man undid the bound gentleman's wrists, then yanked the sack off his face. Vic Stebbins was small, and thick, and sweaty, with dirty blonde hair and tiny fogged up spectacles.

Colm helped Stebbins to his feet and they returned to the car. As they began driving down the hill, Stebbins rifled through the back seat, finding a bottle of brandy from which he took several swigs.

As the car approached the gallery, they could see the window had been smashed in. All the frames along the wall had been removed, and the door to the back room had been torn off its hinges. Colm parked, then he and Stebbins entered the gallery. Van der Vecken was in the back room lying beside one of the ransacked crates. Stebbins turned him over. His face was bruised, but he was still breathing.

"Good to see you old friend," Stebbins said. Stebbins handed Van der Vecken the brandy, and he drank liberally from it.

"I think we're in a bit of a mess," said Van der Vecken. "They knew where the original was, in that crate over there. It was the first thing they took."

"Who else did you tell about the forgery?"

"My wife and Wilhelm," said Van der Vecken. He walked over to a telephone nailed to the side of the wall and dialed.

"Miriam, are you all right? Very well, darling. Worry not, we shall lovingly embrace in just a short while."

Van der Vecken hung up the phone.

"Despite my initial suspicions, my wife has evidently not absconded with the paintings."

"Where does this orator live?"

The three men piled into a car and drove to a brown brick tenement near the docks. They walked into the building, and found the man's room open and unoccupied, with a note to management and his keys atop the table, the only piece of furniture left in the room.

"Planned, then," said Colm. "He may still be in the city. Were there other places that allowed him to hold meetings?"

"A cafe down the road."

"Very well. We may locate one of his associates that way."

The three men walked down the road to the small cafe, where a half dozen men read newspapers and drank coffee on round tables.

"Any of them?"

"The one with the hat attended a meeting last month," said Van der Vecken, pointing to a man with a thin mustache, who wore an ornate, dark red suit jacket and matching bowler hat. Colm walked over to the man.

"I'm looking for a man named Wilhelm."

"Rubbish man, rubbish ideas."

"I'm not the police. Whatever his ideological leanings, he's a thief first and foremost. He stole a gallery's worth of art and skipped his apartment."

"He's gone, then?"

"Should he have told you first?"

"He was making collections for a worker's union. Took a month's wages from me."

"Well, if you'd like to have an unpleasant conversation with him about it, I can place him on the ground first."

"My name's Bennett, I'll lead the way."

The four men stormed the crowded street, weaving through bystanders until they came to another gray, crumbling tenement. They ascended four sets of stairs, and found the third door on the right. Bennett knocked on it.

When Wilhelm answered, Colm yanked him beyond the threshold and slammed his gun into the man's face. His broken nose gushed blood, and he slunk to his knees. Two voices sounded within.

When another man appeared in the doorway, Colm slammed the pistol into his face, and he fell to the ground. Gunfire emerged from inside, peppering Bennett. He shuddered and collapsed. Colm went low, aimed his pistol around the frame and fired. Then he watched for the return fire that struck the hallway's back wall. Judging the assailant's position in the room, Colm stood and shot twice through the room's wall. A body dropped inside.

Colm tied the two assailants in the hallway with ropes, then went into the small room and inspected the dead man. There was no sign of the paintings within. Colm walked over to Wilhelm and yanked him up by his hair.

"Give up the ghost," said Colm.

Wilhelm gave the address of the warehouse where the paintings were being kept. Shortly after, the police arrived at the apartment. The men explained the situation to the best of their ability, then retrieved the paintings from the warehouse. Colm went back to his flat, dialed his report in to Edith and then fell asleep.

PART XVI

Colm's next assignment would take him into the wilderness as the weather was turning. Two girls had gone missing from a small fishing village along the coast called Abadie. With local authorities unable to locate his daughters, Melanie and Abigail, Bruce Baffier had contacted the agency as his last, best hope.

Through a misty snowstorm, Colm travelled by sled dog team to the town's sturdy, wooden trading outpost. Beyond its walls was a single row of buildings constituting main street. A perpendicular road through its center led to inland dwellings on the left, while the cannery and fishing areas were on the right.

Colm shook his snow-drenched raccoon coat clean before he entered the building. Behind the counter was Oliver Calvet, the grizzled hunter who owned the establishment. He had a well-trimmed white beard that matched the thick head of hair above his stringy, tough face.

"You're gonna figure out what they couldn't, huh?" Oliver asked.

"Two lives are worth another set of eyes."

Oliver nodded.

"Where's Baffier's property?"

"Where the road forks left, yonder. Hardly see him anymore. Other folks in town talk about him like the punch line to some tragic myth. The story's already told."

Colm stepped out of the outpost and walked through town. There were lights burning in some of the buildings, but he didn't enter any of them. He turned left up the road, following it through sparse forest to the wooden cabin tucked beneath the shelf of a low cliff.

Colm knocked on the door and Bruce Baffier opened it. He had thinning, dirty blonde hair and a red face. He wore a filthy white button up shirt and brown pants. Colm walked inside and hung his coat over the fireplace in the living room, then passed through its threshold into the kitchen where Baffier served him coffee and beef stew.

"Must have been quite the trip."

"Hopefully the storm lets up. I'd like to get started in the morning."

"I'd appreciate that."

"Anything you can tell me about when you last saw the girls?"

"Melanie was going on about how Abigail didn't play right. There were rules you see, to the kingdom they had made. Melanie was the tyrant, Abigail was some kind of gallant knight I guess. Talked about her birthright. Like it was a place they were fighting over. Must have got it from one of those."

Baffier gestured to some books on a shelf in the living room and laughed. There was a picture there of Baffier, his deceased wife, and his two blonde daughters in white formal wear against black curtains. When they were done eating, Baffier made up a place for Colm on the sofa near the fireplace. Then he retired to his bedroom, and both men fell asleep.

In the morning, the snow had abated. Colm put on his fur coat and ventured into the woods. He followed the sound of rushing water to a stream. He followed it for about an hour to where the ground elevated and formed a slight waterfall.

Colm stepped behind the curtain. A stony lip within provided enough room for a person to squat down, so he did, and examined the walls. Someone had taken a piece of chalk to the wall and drawn a picture of a castle inside a hole in the earth. The hole was near what looked like two trees fallen against another one. A picture of the waterfall was to the castle's distant right.

Colm left the cavern, following the directions of the crude diagram into the woods. After an hour, he saw two trees fallen against a third. He began scanning the ground, and eventually found a depression between a stone shelf and the ground. There was enough room to ease himself below.

As he pushed himself through the dirt barricade, he saw light shining within. Ahead was a small cavern, where a blind man with ragged wisps of black hair, clothed in rags, sat cross-legged in front of a cauldron. He had assorted supplies to his left and right, clothing and tins of food, with rows of waxy candles burning along the walls. There was another entryway behind him that went deeper into the cave.

"Why have you disturbed this place?" asked the blind man.

"Two girls have gone missing. I found a drawing. It led me here."

"Sit with me, and we may find them yet."

"How?"

"Sit with me."

Colm walked over to the blind man and sat down in front of his cauldron. The blind man grabbed a can of herbs, and poured them into a mortar, which he ground down with a pestle. The blind man lit a stick with a match and touched the burning stick to the mortar and breathed in deeply. He passed the mortar to Colm.

"Picture the two girls."

Colm inhaled the fumes.

"A trader often passes along the road beyond this next passage. He will have seen them."

Colm stood, and walked into the next corridor, climbing a series of rocks into another area of woods. Colm found the dirt road ahead of him and waited. After an hour, he heard the sound of hooves.

A man on horseback with long gray hair appeared. Colm waved him down.

"I'm looking for two missing girls."

"Some Mennonites showed up at a trading post an hour that way. They might have seen them."

The man lifted Colm onto the horse behind him, and they rode off. When Colm entered the trading post, he asked the man behind the desk about the Mennonites. He told him to check a hotel just down the road, situated along the face of a cliff. Colm walked into the hotel, and was told by the owner, a brown-haired man in a white suit and spectacles, that the Mennonites had assembled in an upstairs room.

Colm knocked on the door. A Mennonite in a straw hat greeted him. Colm asked him about the girls, displaying a photograph of them he had gotten in the red envelope from Beringar. The Mennonite walked into the hallway and then into the next room, producing the two girls in traditional black dresses. They had evidently stumbled onto the Mennonites' distant farm some weeks back.

The Mennonites had returned this way by pure happenstance to attend the funeral of a relation. Though he wouldn't release the girls into Colm's custody, the Mennonite urged him to contact Bruce so he might claim them.

Colm went to the trading post and dialed Oliver's store from there. Oliver promised to fetch Bruce. Bruce and Oliver arrived on horseback a few hours later. The girls were subdued and unable to recall the events surrounding their disappearance but were exceedingly happy to see their father. The group spent the evening at the hotel, then returned to the Baffier farm the next morning. Colm returned to Montreal that afternoon.

PART XVII

Colm's next assignment had him again braving the Canadian wilderness. To his delight, it was near a railway station so he avoided the blistering cold of another sled dog trip. The town of Brymner was situated around a timber mill that had become important in recent years as the government had ear-marked the surrounding land for a highway. The mayor, a man named Gabriel Cloutier, had hired the enquiry service to keep an eye on a labor organizer named Declan Bergeron. Cloutier feared Bergeron's recent efforts to unionize the workers might prove an obstacle to the development process.

Colm met the mayor in the municipal office located along the snowy main drag of the town, situated amidst a medley of small brick shops. His blonde-haired secretary, a Ms. Ryerson, escorted Colm from her office nook beside the wooden staircase on the first floor to Cloutier's second floor office. In addition to the elegant oak desk and cabinets beside the window, it possessed a fireplace and two chairs where Colm and Cloutier had their meeting. Cloutier wore suspenders over a white dress shirt, black pants and shimmering dark shoes. He was partially bald, with a lean, serious face and a ragged beard. He stared at the fire as he drank his whiskey.

"Of course I see it from their side," said Cloutier. "Or else I wouldn't be able to circumvent their intentions. What are they appealing to, exactly?"

"A shared sense of obligation."

"Regardless of its origin, this is a predicament with two sides. If they're appealing to our mutual humanity, they are correct to, inasmuch as a man accrues responsibilities, and must occasionally perform dreadful tasks in their debt. I recognize their situation, but it won't change the things I have to do. This man, Bergeron, is scheduled to speak at the pool hall down the road this evening. I'd like you to report back on the event, and his activities afterwards. Following that, we can further discuss your suggestions for eliminating the threat. I understand you've had success with these sorts of investigations in the past."

"Different men, in different parts of the world."

"One man lives in the world. With the same motives and vulnerabilities in whatever form you encounter him. Untangle this one with efficiency."

Colm nodded and left.

The motel was across the road. He dropped his haversack there in a small wooden room on the first floor that had a good view of the mayor's office. Then he slept on the lumpy bed for a few hours. When it was dark, he made his way down the road to the pool hall, where an outdoor crowd was filtering in. The timber mill workers had just clocked out, and were enjoying their first drinks spread along the row of tables against the left wall and bar area on the right. They had hard faces and dirty, dark coats. Ancient pain animated their movements, the kind that hollows out hope but cruelly spares the host its life.

Declan had on a long brown coat and a black scarf. He had shaggy black hair, sharp cheekbones and gleaming blue eyes. In the brief conversations he had with the men around him he possessed an infectious vivacity. After the men went through another round of drinks, Declan waved his hand and quieted the crowd.

"Gentlemen! You know me. You've heard me labor these points time and again. We are united here on your behalf. They call us agitators. I say what agitates them is their conscience. I say these are good men too. And it is your Christian duty to remind them of their obligations to the human race. The world manufactures artificial separations between us. But it is one race of men that yearns and bleeds. That leads the yoke and yanks the levers. That calls and answers. And what is it you ask of these they call your betters? Name your egregious demands! Decent wages, decent working conditions. Because you have a third desire. One of brotherhood and fraternity and purpose. The kind you have already found in that timber mill. This is not some bloodthirsty negotiation. It is a quarrel between brethren, united by intention. The intention to clear the wilderness beyond, and erect a shining new monument to God's progress. You want this, they want this. They must simply be made aware. And so to anoint their blind eyes with the gift of sight, we will unite. We will lay down our tools, and speak the truth that blossoms from our hearts. And when these demands are met, we shall join hands once more in brotherhood as we march forward into this glorious century..."

It was unclear where the gunshot came from, or its true aim, but a man near Bergeron dropped dead. The crowd erupted, pushing one another down as they poured into the street. A few old squabbles reignited and a handful of patrons were left brawling in the tavern as it cleared out. The dead man was an American named Smokey. He had been in town for just a few days.

The Police Chief, Benjamin Gagnon, arrived a few moments later with his two deputies, Cumber and Hastings. Gagnon was a large, burly man with a thick brown beard, curious eyes and an even thicker fur coat that matched those belonging to his compatriots. Cumber was squat and heavy, with a black handlebar mustache.

Hastings was a lanky redhead.

The trio arrested Bergeron for inciting a riot and for membership in an unlawful organization, as they found his membership card for an American socialist group. They hauled him off to the jail at police headquarters, located at the far end of main street. Colm followed the men there and requested an audience with Gagnon.

Gagnon led Colm into a back room used for interrogations, and had Colm take a seat at its central table. Gagnon removed his fur coat, revealing his dark blue button-up uniform, before he sat down in front of Colm.

"Cloutier hired you."

"He didn't tell you?"

"We haven't spoken in weeks. It's a slap in the face, you understand? He thinks we aren't handling this to his satisfaction. That we're letting the radical elements steer the course of events."

"A problem that was conveniently solved this evening."

"You're asking if we gave a man's life to break a looming strike?"

"I'm remarking on the timing. Will this effectively bring things to an end?"

"If one of his other men doesn't step in. He had a cousin who was part of the group tonight, Lutovsky. Ambitious, well-liked. Might be a problem. We're keeping an eye on him."

"Where's he staying?"

"I appreciate you introducing yourself. We have some paperwork to complete now."

"Can I speak to Bergeron?"

"Not tonight."

Gagnon led Colm out of the station. He went back to his room.

Lacking any leads, he ventured to the timber mill the next morning, which was on the outskirts of town. A pile of logs lay in a ditch to the left of the large wooden building where the saw blazed an eerie whine. As he arrived, so did two more trucks filled with uncut logs. Men emerged from the truck and used hooks from the flatbed to dump the logs into the pile. There was a privy to the right of the main building. As a thin, bald worker in a gray coat emerged from it, Colm approached him and asked about Lutovsky.

"I'm not with Chief Gagnon," Colm said. "I might be able to help your pal Bergeron."

"He's staying in a back room behind the Laughing Walrus pub. The owner's a sympathizer."

Colm thanked him and went to find the pub.

Besides the stout blonde bartender, the unvarnished wooden room was deserted. Colm ordered a gin and sat at a side table. He took his time finishing it and went to the bar for another.

"I'd be interested in a friendly conversation with Lutovsky."

Colm had fashioned a card proclaiming his membership in the United Workers of Canada, which he demonstrated to the barkeep. The barkeep poured Colm another gin, then went into the back room. A few minutes later, Lutovsky appeared. He was the runt to Bergeron's champion breed. He possessed the same vague handsomeness, blue eyes and sharp cheekbones below a more refined, short brown haircut, but lacked his cousin's confidence. He obtained a whiskey from the barkeep then sat down in front of Colm. Colm wanted to test how far he was willing to go before he reported back to Cloutier.

"Your cousin has laid the foundation for some important work here," Colm said.

"It's all gone to shit," said Lutovsky.

"You could salvage it. Call for a general strike. It makes the papers. All the other leftist organizations in Quebec will heed the call, rush to your cousin's aid. Legal support. Political favors. If they see a winnable fight here, they'll want to use it to build support for their own local struggles."

"It's all a bit much."

"Well, just know you've got an ally in me. I'm in the motel across the road. Come to me for absolutely anything."

Colm went to his hotel for a brief spell in case he was being followed, then he flitted out the back entrance and over to the mayor's office. There, they sat in the same seats as before, while Colm apprised him of the general situation.

"To maintain the veneer of legality, Lutovsky would have to act first and give your constables an excuse to remove him from the fight."

"You think you can goad him into doing this?" asked Cloutier.

"If that's what you'd like. The problem being if he does act and it's successful, or it fails but inspires the workers to re-organize..."

"Right."

"You've spoken to Gagnon again?" asked Colm.

"Reluctantly."

"What will happen with Bergeron?"

"They'll prosecute him under Code 98, sentence length will depend on the magistrate. Regardless, he'll turn up somewhere else as someone else's problem. Our real issue is, this is a movement he adopted, not created. A swift blow to obliterate the animating spirit of the cause would be best. If not the impulse, then the desire to fulfill the impulse."

The next morning, the mayor got his wish.

Colm noticed a small crowd had gathered in front of the police station just after sunrise. He ambled over to where a few shopkeepers and mill workers playing hooky were speaking in hushed tones. Colm asked what happened.

"Bergeron hung himself," said one of the men, producing a scoff in several of his companions.

Colm rushed over to the Laughing Walrus. Lutovsky

was seated at one of the tables, downing glass after glass of whiskey. Colm sat down in front of him.

"Awful news."

Lutovsky nodded.

"What will you do?"

"I thought he was just going to get back up and do it again. No matter how many times they knocked him down he always stood back up. Maybe this means I have to be the one to stand up."

Lutovsky finished his whiskey and pushed the bottle forward. He stood and walked to his room. Colm went to the mayor's office. The mayor was evidently on an important phone call regarding other portions of the highway project, so Colm waited downstairs with Ms. Ryerson. Eventually, the door opened upstairs, and Cloutier invited Colm to join him.

Colm stood against the window, Cloutier remained seated at his desk.

"Pleased with the news?" Colm asked.

"It was a delightful development. Helped reinvigorate my belief in my own people."

"I spoke with Lutovsky. He's been reinvigorated as well. It seems you'll get your wish."

"When?"

"Likely the next few days. The situation will come to a head, and you can deal a second devastating blow to the movement. Peace will be restored to the kingdom."

"Keep me informed," Cloutier said.

Colm left the office and went back to his hotel.

He checked the pubs that evening to glean any new developments. He found the busiest one on the far end of town, which was about half full with workers. He ordered a gin there and kept his ears open. He was nearly done for the night when Deputy Hastings stumbled in with a thin, dark-haired prostitute who wore furs over her black dress. They took a seat close to the back entrance. They had two drinks and then left. Colm followed them.

They went to a three-story wooden building on a street parallel to the main road. They stayed there for an hour, then Hastings stumbled out by himself. Colm went inside the establishment, which was part boarding house and part brothel. The madam was an older, redheaded woman sitting on a blue sofa in the small front room. Colm told her Deputy Hastings had recommended a dark-haired beauty he'd spent some time with. He paid the madam her coinage, and then strolled up the stairs to Ramona's room.

She was preparing for bed when he entered, already in her white night dress, her make-up and wig removed. Her real hair was short and auburn.

"Can we talk first?"

Ramona shrugged her shoulders. Colm sat down beside her.

"I saw you with my friend earlier."

"Mr. Hastings?"

"That's right."

"You're with the police?"

"No, no. We just have a few drinks now and again. You like him?"

"He's fine, mostly."

"He'll be pleased to hear that."

"No, I mean...he's better than fine. It's been a long day."

"He's been having a few of those himself lately," said Colm.

"To hear him talk of it, yeah," she said.

"You don't know the half of it."

"What don't I know?"

"I couldn't tell you, I'd get my head bashed in. It's scandalous, to say the least."

"Now you simply must tell me," she said. "Hastings trusts me. We talk all the time."

"It's about the Bergeron bloke," said Colm.

"What about him?"

"What's he told you already?"

"Just that he had an accident."

"That's right," Colm laughed.

"And that his brother's gonna have one pretty soon, too."

Colm nodded.

"Tomorrow night, right?" Colm said.

"Not what I heard," said Ramona.

"Right, I'm getting my days mixed up," Colm said, fishing. "He said that two days ago..."

"Right, so he's been getting a load on tonight in anticipation."

"Speaking of which, I've got a bottle of premium whiskey in room," said Colm. "Will you hang on for me?"

"I might be asleep," said Ramona.

"I'll be quick."

Colm left the boarding house and rushed over to the Laughing Walrus. There were a few timber workers drunk inside, but it was mostly empty. Colm went to the back room and knocked. Lutovsky opened the door. Colm stepped inside the room, which more closely resembled a wash closet with a bed and sink.

"They're coming to kill you tonight," said Colm.

"I don't care," said Lutovsky.

"This fight is lost," said Colm. "If you want to honor your brother's memory, you should do it somewhere else. The battle is not the war."

"This battle is my war," said Lutovsky. "It's all I have left of him."

"It's a pointless way to die."

"So be it," said Lutovsky.

Colm fumed. He slammed the door shut as he left.

He went back to his hotel, dug out a bottle of gin and got drunk. He stumbled outside with the bottle and watched the Laughing Walrus from a distance. Eventually, he saw two men in furs and sackcloth hoods approach the pub. He heard Lutovsky scream inside as he was dragged through the back entrance of the building. Then he heard three gunshots.

Colm went back into the hotel and fell asleep.

In the morning, he went to the mayor's office one last time. Ms. Ryerson told him the mayor was out but thanked him for his services. She handed Colm a check and said his business there was concluded. He grabbed his haversack from his hotel room.

A light snow was falling as he walked to the train station on the outskirts of town. The last ten years and their unending cycle of death and futility prodded at him. And yet despite his self-pity, the swirl of snow persisted, as did the bird songs from the barren trees, as did his ceaseless march into the hands of the laughing Fates.

PART XVIII

After the dispiriting events in Brymner, Colm spent a few dismal weeks isolated in his flat in Montreal. He read cheap novels, played endless hands of solitaire, drank too much rye whiskey and left the room only at night to fetch supplies from the nearby market just before it closed.

During one of these stumbling excursions, a blonde woman in a white cloche and a matching, modest dress handed him a pamphlet for a local temperance meeting hosted by the Daughters of the Empty Jug. She introduced herself as Gertrude Barbaroux. She had soft brown eyes and extolled her chapter's virtues with a half-smirk that came off as endearing.

"I fear these words fall on an empty choir," she said, tilting Colm's gaze back towards her with a gentle touch of the hand.

"Not quite, though the audience is certainly slumped low in their seats."

"Does it add to the texture of your experience? The drink?"

"That's a bit sentimental," he said.

"You've the eyes for it. Gentle, aching liars."

"They've only just found your acquaintance."

"You save your malicious meanderings for a second meeting?"

"Darling, there are demons in this world. Best not convert the innocent to their cause."

"Better still, convert the wicked back to mine."

"As far as I can tell, you've done just that. Miscreants railing against the fundamental rights of this fine nation."

"Name a greater cause of suffering among the populace."

"I can think of just the one. Life."

"Allow me the opportunity to change your mind," she said. "Come to one of our meetings."

Colm thumbed through the pamphlet.

"Let's say I make it through the whole thing upright."

"I grant you this wild flight of fancy."

"I'd argue it's worth a post-mortem afterwards. At a cafe."

"Surely," she said. "Given your abusive relationship with gravity, it would be an affront to science not to investigate."

"Then I will see you tomorrow evening."

Colm kissed her hand and walked back to his room.

He hadn't heard from the enquiry service in a few weeks and thought to pay Edith a visit the next morning.

"Fortuitous," she said as Colm took the seat in front of her desk. She wore a blue turtleneck over a brown skirt, and her red hair was done up in a bun. "You've saved the company a round of postage, it'll be added to your next stub."

"Who are the unfortunates this go-round?"

"The Evening Duty."

"Someone finally torch that rubbish heap?"

"One of their journalists went missing."

"Narrows it down to anyone who has purchased a paper since the new editor took over."

"It has descended into a bit of salaciousness, I don't think that forfeits the right of their workers to safe passage in the city."

"I'll certainly take money to pretend I agree. Let's see the file."

Edith pushed the red envelope across the desk.

"He was investigating some bootleggers. Small-timers elbowing their way in, Sighle and McGlade."

Colm thumbed past the typed documents to the newspaper clippings Edith had left for him. There was a photograph of two men in black trench coats and bowlers lugging barrels of liquor from a warehouse into a car.

"Can't imagine that was great for business."

"Hardly matters this side of the line, but the Americans waiting for them had fun with it."

"Did they walk free?"

"Barely. Authorities ran them off, found the car but not the men or the liquor."

"Boat waiting for them?"

"Probably," she said. "But the journalist, Fearghal Carrick, goes missing a few days later. 'Pursuing another line of enquiry,' is all he had time to tell his editor before he chased what was probably his final lead."

"You're doubting the mercy of these upstanding gentlemen?"

Edith concealed a smile and turned back to her typewriter.

"I look forward to speaking with you again once you've accomplished these tasks to my satisfaction," she said.

"I'll bring back what's left of him. Should be a good deal intact, with the weather we've been having."

Colm stood to leave but stopped himself at the door.

"Am I a drunkard?" he asked her.

"You're a pint with a pulse."

"Worth looking into?"

"It catches up to most men before they think to look back. And it's an ugly day when it does."

The Evening Duty offices were a short cab ride away. Heavy sunlight slanted through the far windows against the dozen or so suited men crowded in the bull pen, their desks littered with documents, tapping typewriters and cigarette smoke.

The editor was a man named Kerry Carlow. He was broad-shouldered, with slicked-back hair and a fine gray suit. He met Colm beside the secretary's desk, and led him over to Fearghal's, reiterating most of Edith's notes along the way.

"Seems like something your staff would love to take a crack at. One of your own and all."

"That'd be a way to get an answer, certainly. Maybe not the right one."

"You suspect one of them?"

"We had a staff turnover a year back, my position included."

"I'm aware," said Colm.

"Three heads. My predecessor falls on his sword, as do two of the men involved in a captivating tale wherein a boat owned by a Montreal city councilman is seized downriver with machine guns and liquor. This racy jaunt is buried in red ink. And after the bloodbath, one man is left standing."

"Fearghal."

"They know us. And they know our hands our tied."

"I'd like to start with these two. Sighle and McGlade."

"Their daylight racket was wholesale timber here," Carlow pointed to an address on the second page of notes. "Sighle's father owned it. Hasn't re-opened since the story ran. The duo shared a house up until that point, listed on the next page. Vacated, as well. Fearghal hadn't found their new address yet."

Colm shook hands with Carlow and set off for the docks. He located the abandoned office, two desolate wooden rooms filled with an empty desk and shelves. There was a hollow place in the floorboards at the back wall, but when he looked within, it had been cleaned out. Their house, a blue single-story shotgun shack a few blocks away, was similarly wiped of any evidence.

He sat on the steps of the residence, smoking a cigarette as he checked the paperwork for another lead. He decided on Fearghal's apartment. A short cab ride deposited him in front of the two-story white building.

The man's sister, Eula, a curly dark-haired woman holding a crying infant, opened the door. Colm introduced himself.

"I'm with the paper."

"I know everyone with the paper."

"That's the problem, isn't it?"

Eula nodded and they walked through the anteroom, crossing the long hall that divided the first floor of the house before entering the kitchen. They took a seat there, where she continued spooning her baby gruel as Colm asked her for any details that might help.

"He had a superstitious nature. Thought to speak of things might alter the energy surrounding events."

"Where'd he do his work?"

"The study. Far end of the hall," she said.

Bookshelves covered two walls. There was a desk with a typewriter and a smaller shelf against the far side of the room. Colm stepped over to the table and began leafing through Fearghal's notes. The newest ones were about a horse-racing scandal, they were written in pen. The shelf contained leather-bound binders labelled and sorted by year.

Colm took down the three binders corresponding to the previous year, and found they were sub-divided by case. He stopped at the one labelled "Blood Feud." The typed notes within detailed a conflict between two city council members, Edward Webster, a stoic Englishman from a family of prominent shipbuilders, and Frederick Cazale, a backwoods Frenchman. Their struggle stemmed from Cazale's decisive vote against awarding a port contract to Webster's relations.

Fearghal had apparently discovered Webster's ships

were entering American waters to off-load liquor. The real issue was Cazale's attempt to do the same thing. Webster had developed a relationship with a man named Virgil Lavoie who had a monopoly on illicit water traffic in the area. Those violating his sovereignty had all reputedly met gruesome ends. The nearest town to Virgil's property was a place called Hewitt's Breach. Colm figured that would be the place to begin his investigation in the morning. He gathered the binders and went back into the kitchen.

"These will help enormously," Colm said. Eula nodded. Colm left for his apartment.

There, he spruced himself up for the evening's temperance society meeting.

It was held in a Methodist church two blocks from Colm's apartment. The pews were less than a quarter full, mostly older women in plain dresses. Gertrude wore a dark red one with a black belt that evening. Her hair flowed at the shoulders and she held her hands close together as if the speech were either prayer or spell. She spoke passionately of her life, the troubles of her parents after she'd come to Montreal, and what the drink had done to her father's already diminished state before he dimmed completely.

"So I say to you, sisters, these men sell trojan horses in bottles," she concluded. "Their spirits lock arms with specters, and they seek a third as they dawdle down to hell."

Following her speech, two other women spoke of their family's troubles. The second one, a meek dark-hair of middle-age, recounted her husband's murder during a pub fight, and how she struggled to survive with her two children afterwards.

Afterwards, the women made preliminary plans to protest a local distillery that officially sold to Caribbean countries, but whose products were re-routed back to America once they'd left Canadian waters. After Gertrude was done speaking with the remaining women individually, they filed out of the church. She stood in the aisle beside Colm.

"Did it scrape your conscience?"

"What heart wouldn't bend?"

"And yet you've a flask beneath your coat."

"I needed to hear all sides out before making any hasty judgments. It's a nice flask, after all. However well-intentioned it was, they've made a mess of the whole thing. Outlawing it created a market they couldn't regulate."

"Suppose I said you were right."

"It still wouldn't undo what happened to your father. It's small against the big picture maybe, but it's a trick of perspective isn't it? You're down where the shadow it throws is everything. Coffee, then?"

She nodded. They left the church and walked to a cafe nearby. Colm brought two coffees over to a table by the window where they watched foot traffic pass along brick storefronts.

"You're not a full-time crusader."

"No, I teach school," she said.

"They're fond of you."

"They get used to you. Dependency. There's a difference."

"You could make the whole world ugly that way. What would love look like? A love that doesn't come from a rational impulse for survival. Or irrational devotion to some obscure inner working of the body."

"That doesn't sound like something that exists," she said. "And yet we're built to desire. So one marches along or one falters. When I saw you that first night in the market, you weren't nervous. Not like you are around me."

"Makes you question this whole tryst."

"I'd like to see you that way again," she said.

"Maybe next time."

"It's quite late."

Colm walked her to an apartment building much like his own. They stopped outside of the entrance. He went to shake her hand, and she pulled him close for a friendly hug. She went inside, and he walked home.

He practiced moderation that evening in her honor, drifting into dreamless slumber as he recalled the contours of her chin and her gentle scent slipping away from him in the darkness.

He arranged for a company car and made sure it was one they wouldn't mind losing. Edith handed him the keys to the dark blue Whiskey Six just after sunrise. He drove the whole morning until he reached the small fishing village of Hewitt's Breach along the mouth of Lake Ontario.

At the general store, two old men looked through tackle and fishing lines. Colm asked the shopkeeper, a disinterested youngster with brown hair who was reading a department store catalogue, the best route to Virgil's Cove.

The youngster looked up at Colm with his mention of the name.

"The only people who have any business going there wouldn't require directions."

"I have kin buried up that way. I've no interest in local affairs, just want to pay my respects."

The young man took a piece of paper from behind the counter and drew a map.

"If you think this is me doing you a favor, you're mistaken. If you were somebody I cared for in the slightest I'd have already run you off in the opposite direction."

The young man pushed the paper forward. Colm thanked him and headed outside.

Through a break in the woods beyond the town's last building, a dirt road curved inland. A few miles up, the road almost imperceptibly split, traffic to the next town veering right past a rock outcropping. Colm followed the map's instructions, maneuvering along the boulders and finding a smaller path that slung up a cliff face that opened its left flank to the water.

The road sunk again, passing along another screen of

trees into a midday darkness of enveloping trunks. The posts of the bridge rose up from the road. When Colm reached them, he could see where the bridge had fallen to the sliver of water snaking below.

Colm got out of the car and took a closer look at the stream. He could see a thin rope of land curl along the left cliff face, and thought he might be able to reach it through the woods. He drove the car as far as he could into the trees and covered it with branches. Afterwards, he ambled down the slope until he got to the beach.

He turned right, walking until the bridge was overhead. He kept going until the bed got shallow enough to cross. When he was on the other side, he followed the sand for a mile until he located an animal trail back up the elevation into the woods. He found the road again, and when he cast a glance across the chasm, he could see the two men following him had discovered the car. He moved ahead to where the road dipped down, but the rock walls and trees remained tall on either side of him.

It opened up onto a bay, where about a mile off, the wooded, triangular edge of Virgil's Cove rose from the fog along the water. Colm searched the lip of sand, and found a small boat hidden in the brush. He dragged it into the water and used a single oar to propel it to the far shore. As he got there, he looked back at his pursuers on the other side as they walked to another section of the beach.

He stashed the boat behind another bush and walked a mile along a rough foot path. Where the land tilted low and the trees began to clear, he found the rickety wooden buildings that formed the outer rim of the farm. The main house was surrounded by acres of rye fields. Two men with shotguns patrolled it.

Colm encircled the property, staying low in the trees until he found a path on the other side. He followed it to a trio of small motorboats rigged to a dock. There was a can of petrol in the middle boat. He sprayed two of the boats with gasoline, then started the third. He struck two matches and lit the boats on fire. Then he drove off, half-circling the island.

He found a landing mid-way and concealed the boat in some thorny brush. Then he ascended the sandy cliff-side, drawing his pistol as he approached the house. The men with shotguns were gone. He opened the back door, and walked into the kitchen, where Virgil Lavoie was drinking a cup of tea and reading a newspaper.

"This is an unfortunate situation you've stumbled into," Virgil said. He was a thin, older gentleman with gray hair and a red-checkered flannel. "Let me allow you the opportunity to stumble back out of it."

"Fearghal Carrick," Colm said. "The journalist."

"Not who we were after."

"Cazale hired those bootleggers, Sighle and McGlade, to infringe on your monopoly. You had them killed. Fearghal was in the wrong place."

"Who are you exactly?"

"Yes or no. A nod would suffice."

"Who hired you?"

"Convince me there's a deal to be made."

"If Cazale did, let me tell you, you're betting on a losing horse."

Virgil seemed to be considering his options, thinking about how much to reveal.

"Let's say I could cut him in. Allow him passage through the bay, storage for his goods."

"In exchange for the cost of the two men he just lost," Colm said, fishing for an admission.

"There would have to be other concessions. On his end, council business. Two dead backwoods..."

That was enough for Colm. He shot Virgil once in the stomach and once in the head, then walked through the back door and stumbled down the beach to the boat. He started it, then took a jagged path up the coastline, where he found a place to abandon the vessel. The car was clean, he didn't bother going back for it.

He hired a taxi from a petrol station further up the road, and took it all the way back to Montreal. If he was linked to the murder, he might face reprisal from one of Virgil's associates. But Cazale would be the obvious suspect.

Back in his apartment, Colm typed up a letter to Webster to nudge suspicion in the right direction, antagonizing him on behalf of Cazale. He handled it with gloves and posted it without a return address. He contacted the police with an anonymous tip suggesting Cazale's life was in danger. In separate notes to Edith and Kerry Carlow he confided his suspicion that Virgil had murdered the journalist. He cited a new, manufactured portion of Fearghal's binder, while concealing his true actions.

A few days later, news came of the attack on Cazale's compound. Two pistol-wielding assassins in balaclavas were apprehended outside of his house. In police custody, they immediately gave up Webster as part of the deal. Their confessions also included the final resting spot of Sighle, McGlade, and Fearghal, a shallow grave in the woods of Virgil's cove.

It was a messy solution that required more subterfuge than Colm would have liked, but he settled it to his satisfaction with Edith and the Evening Duty by providing the binders and taking strictly confidential credit for the police tip. Through the enquiry service, Carlow invited Colm for a drink, which he asked Edith to politely decline. He was fearful the man's instincts might uncover what really happened.

Instead, he called on Gertrude. He met her at another cafe nearby, with simple wood floors and tables. They didn't talk much; he was too unwilling to reveal enough about himself to instill any trust in her. All his polite redirections led nowhere, and their encounter stuttered into silence. She gave him a stiff hug and walked off. He finished his cigarette and returned to his apartment.

PART XIX

Pagnier started as a small timber mining community. After Prohibition, it became the base of operations for a booze-smuggling criminal syndicate run by Baciu Ondruska. Ondruska's family was displaced from Yugoslavia during the Balkan Wars. He and his cousin, Pejic, started out by selling stolen liquor for one of the larger outfits in Quebec before branching out into moonshine production on their own.

They had an understanding with local authorities that held as long as long as more egregious crimes didn't occur. Baciu either dutifully met his obligations or made serious efforts to bury his transgressions. However, his origins in the racket, the man he murdered to obtain his independence, would become the inflection point preceding his final days.

Baciu's partner in his youth was a man named Rufus Ploiffe. Baciu was a petty thief, whom Ploiffe saved from a short jail sentence in exchange for help hijacking booze shipments headed into the United States. Ploiffe was under the assumption this was a long-term arrangement, which it was, until the Ondruskas wrestled control of Pagnier's distilleries from a dying clan of mountain grifters. Shortly afterwards, Rufus Ploiffe disappeared.

Ploiffe was related by marriage to a German banker named Cecil Graffe. Though Ploiffe and his wife had long since separated, her brother sought restitution for the tidy sum with which Ploiffe had absconded. To that effect, Graffe contacted Beringar's Enquiry Service. Colm once again found himself headed into the shivering backwoods of Canada, this time via company automobile, a white Duesenberg Model A.

Pagnier's main drag was two semi-circles of wooden buildings eyeing one another across a field of snow. The hotel was two buildings from the train stop, itself a short distance from a steep cliff that dropped into forest to the town's right, eventually leading to Lake St. Jean.

The hotelier was not unfriendly, a grim woman with gray hair who favored dark-colored dresses and was always listening to serialized radio dramas whenever Colm happened over to her desk. He asked for the nearest tavern, and she replied there was just the one, two doors down, along the same side of the street.

Colm went there that evening, ordered a light meal and attempted to establish himself as a hapless salesman traveling through. He asked the bartender, a squat, animated fellow with neat, blondish-brown hair named Gilbert, about locals who might be interested in his wares. On this trip, he happened to be selling luxury travel by rail or sea to a series of exotic locations.

"Not sure you'll find many takers here, sir. This is a place one goes after life has already been exciting enough."

"Surely there must be some interested citizens. Local businessmen or the like."

"Only one business around these parts," said Gilbert.

"Do you happen to be selling it behind the bar?"

Gilbert grinned sheepishly.

"You're quite the entrepreneur."

"It's not my establishment," he said.

"Who owns it?"

"Mr. Ondruska."

"Mr. Ondruska," said Colm, lighting a cigarette. "Mr. Ondruska wouldn't be interested in some of these travel opportunities?"

"I think you'd hazard your health with the question."

"Well, I appreciate the warning. If he comes in here, I'll be sure not to broach the subject."

"Shouldn't worry about that. He never makes it off his property these days."

"He never comes into town for anything?"

"One of his boys will come in sometimes. You don't want to sell them anything either."

"Then I'm glad I spoke to you first, Gilbert. Now I know who to steer clear of."

Colm finished his meal and went back to his room.

The town was in the man's thrall, more questions would probably be a mistake. He'd keep an eye out for one of the underlings as long as it took, and then follow him to the property. He spent another three days eating meals at Gilbert's tavern. When he went in for breakfast on the fourth, there was a blonde-haired man with a boxer's frame in a grey trench coat eating at one of the tables.

As Colm waited for his order at the counter, he asked Gilbert:

"One of them I should steer clear of?"

Gilbert nodded, willfully obscuring his usual talkative demeanor. Colm finished his meal quickly, then went back to the hotel and watched the tavern from his room. The boxer left about a half hour later, went into the general store, and exited with a satchel. He walked over to a blue Colonial automobile and jetted off.

Colm headed downstairs and gave pursuit in the company car.

They drove a few miles up the road, and the Colonial turned onto a rough track that receded into the woods. That road eventually snaked left up a hill onto a flat plateau where Baciu's land rested against more woodlands.

Colm discovered this last part on foot, abandoning his own car some distance down the incline for fear of discovery. He watched the boxer park outside, then walk into the second largest of three red-painted buildings.

Colm walked into the woods to begin his initial surveillance of the property, with one hand on his M1911. After about ten minutes hidden behind one of the trees, the man in back of him spoke in an Eastern European accent:

"Friend, please place the weapon on the ground."

Colm turned and saw the man pointing a pistol at him. He was thicker and taller than the other fellow from the bar, with short dark hair and the same kind of grey trench coat. Colm placed his gun on the ground. The man made a motion for Colm to walk towards the house, which he did. Colm heard him pick the gun up from the ground as he cleared the tree-line into the lot.

They walked over to the largest building.

"Balan, open the door."

The blonde-haired boxer from the bar opened it.

There were crates of booze in two massive rows against either wall. The boxer grabbed a chair, then placed it in front of one of the posts by the right wall of booze. Colm sat in it, then the boxer tied his hands.

The man who abducted him left and returned with another dark-haired man. This one was lankier, with more presence than the other two. A neck tattoo showed just above the collar of his fur coat.

"You arrive with friendly designs?" the man in fur asked, his accent matching the other's.

"Not so friendly," said the abductor. He handed the man in fur the M1911.

"Who sends you this way?" asked the man in fur.

"Are you Baciu?" Colm asked.

Baciu nodded.

"Your name then?"

Colm shook his head.

Baciu nodded. The boxer hit Colm in the stomach. It flared in agony.

"Once more, maybe? I find this occasionally makes people more talkative."

The boxer punched Colm twice more in the stomach.

"Face next. You have someone you need to stay pretty for?"

Colm shook his head.

The boxer hit him in the jaw. A stinging dizziness sent his vision sideways.

"Kill him?" asked the boxer.

Baciu shook his head.

"This man makes a house call unannounced, therefore he owes me a pleasant conversation. It's called decorum."

Baciu lifted Colm up by the hair and slapped him across the face.

"Bring Mable out."

The boxer nodded, then walked behind one of the rows of booze. Colm heard a stall door swing open. The boxer led a cougar out with a rope leash.

"Let's get you in a talking mood," said Baciu. The abductor lifted Colm to his feet and prodded him out the back entrance. They walked across the lot and into the woods until the path dropped slightly and cleared some. There was a razor wire enclosure around what appeared to be a flat, open area.

Baciu pulled up a stake, and the party walked into it.

The flat area was not flat, but in fact, overlooking an open-tunnel system of mud-walled warrens.

"You go in one end, Mable here goes in the other. You talk to me, or you end up meeting her somewhere in the middle."

Baciu pushed Colm over the ledge, and he fell face first in the mud. Colm stood and stumbled forward a few steps. The walls weren't as high as the trenches in France, just barely too tall to climb out of without difficulty.

He walked to the end of the row, then took a right,

stumbling over a mauled corpse. He stifled his nausea and ransacked the body, finding a hunting knife in the man's stiff fingers. He used it to slice through his ropes, and kept walking. He heard the cougar growling to the pathway right, so he took a left, and then another right, where the alley dead ended.

He started climbing the wall, and almost got over the top, but then two shots clipped the ledge near his head and he dropped down. He turned to walk the trail back to the entrance and heard the cougar growl just before it sprung towards him.

He lifted one arm as he fell backwards. The cougar bit into it as Colm stabbed into the beast's head and throat over and over again. The teeth loosened and the beast pulled away. It slunk its head and paws down, breathing a few more shallow breaths before it stopped moving.

Colm's aching arm was soaking the snow with blood. He used his good one to slide himself beneath the cougar.

He heard one of the underlings approach. It was the boxer. When he stooped low to lift the cougar from Colm, Colm stabbed him in the neck. The boxer stumbled backwards and sat down against the wall of the trench. Colm slid out from underneath the beast, grabbed the man's gun and shot him through the head.

There was movement along the ledge where his companion, the abductor, appeared. Colm fired twice, and the man fell flat on his back. His legs lingered over the edge of the warren, where they shook a few more times before he stopped moving.

Colm grabbed the man's foot and yanked him down into the trench. He found his M1911 and holstered the boxer's pistol. He yanked the man's coat off and slung it over his shoulder and placed the knife in his pants. Then he walked over to the end of the maze opposite from where he had entered.

There was an incline where the cougar had walked in. He figured Baciu was either waiting to shoot him, or he'd gone back to the house to phone more of his men. He'd do the latter eventually anyway, so it was either die fast with a headshot or wait until he was surrounded.

He smeared the coat in the mud to weigh it down then stepped onto the incline. He tossed it to the right side of the entrance as he ran up the left and kept his pistol ahead of him. There was no one there. He walked the rim of the ledge to the razor wire entrance and pried the door open.

Colm followed the path back to the farm. As he neared the open lot in front of the barn, a shot rang out from the top floor of the building beside it. He ran into the woods and cut a path back to where he had stashed the car along the road. He started it, then drove back up the hill to the house. He accelerated and smashed through the front facade of the building. After the shock of the impact wore off, he inched the car forward until the engine was blocking the staircase.

He stepped out of the car as Baciu was walking down the steps. Colm fired twice, forcing him back upstairs. Then he took the spare can of petrol from the back seat and sprayed the upper steps with it. He lit a match and tossed it onto the stream of gasoline. As the smoke seared through the room, Colm got back into the car and reversed out of the hole.

He drove around the other side of the building as Baciu, burning, fled through the back door towards the tree line. Baciu stumbled a few steps into the woods, then collapsed in the snow.

Colm got out of the car and shot him in the head. Then he got back into his vehicle and drove down the mountain road towards town, but didn't stop there. He arrived in Montreal late that evening, staggering into a doctor's office that was bankrolled by the enquiry service.

After he was stitched up, he spent a few days in bed recovering. Waking from a fever dream where he was back in the trenches, he briefly considered a change in occupation. But then the phone rang, and Edith's droll tone insisted he was going to love the next case.

He changed into a dark blue three-piece, holstered his M1911 and headed out the door.

PART XX

For the company Christmas party, Edith had festooned one of the archival rooms with seasonal lights that flung gauzy amber onto the red carpets and wooden walls. There were drinks and food along two tables, and jaunty music flowered from a phonograph beside a few filing cabinets.

It was Colm's first time encountering any other agents on the payroll. Even still, most were off performing duties in various parts of the world. Including Colm, there were three PIs there, as well as Beringar, Edith and Osbourne, the company accountant. Osbourne was a bald, diminutive man who that evening wore a tan sweater vest over a white shirt and brown trousers.

Edith's blue sequin dress dazzled. Beringar was his usual stiff ode to decency in a dark blue tuxedo. The duo spent most of the evening tucked beside the wall, their hands casually grazing one another's. Colm stifled his jealousy with the cold comfort of a fellow PI.

Leola Auden would have been a handful on a normal night, but coming off the Pagnier case, her self-evangelizing martyrdom was doing Colm's head in. Her short blonde hair was crimped to the ear, and she wore a black skirt and a matching men's jacket over her blue blouse.

When Colm went to refill his gin, Rudolph Brueghel broke off from his conversation with Osborne and joined him. Brueghel had neat dark hair, and a somber, unfussy face that matched his black suit.

"Will you be wasting the rest of your evening here?" he asked Colm as he filled a glass of bourbon.

"Fuck no," Colm replied.

They did a few lines of cocaine atop the bathroom sink, then snuck around the block to a nearby brothel. They rented a red-lit room on the second floor. Two prostitutes in dark corsets, a blonde and a brunette named Celia and Doris, poured them absinthe as they lounged in the brown armchairs between the red-sheeted beds. The girls said they were part of a cabaret show on hiatus after an arson claimed their theater mid-performance.

"Jilted lover of the new girl," said Celia, kissing Colm.

"It was fucking bedlam in there," drawled Doris as she drained the last of her drink. "All shrieks and elbows. Nearly ended up a smear on someone's shoe."

Colm found himself on one of the beds with Celia, but he'd overestimated his tolerance and passed out shortly after. A few hours before dawn, Beringar shook him awake. He looked over at the naked, dark-haired woman with the knife sticking out of her head.

They wrapped her in the bedsheets. Colm stepped onto the landing and saw the lithe French madam in the pale yellow shift thumb through a novel downstairs. Brueghel tossed Doris' body through the room's side window, and they followed her out the same way. As they drove off in Brueghel's grey Studebaker, he told Colm about an abandoned factory nearby with a furnace they could use. They stopped at Brueghel's apartment so he could get the lighter fluid.

Lit by starlight through boarded windows, the warehouse was dismal and sooty, filled with rotting crates and pallets. Beside the hulking brute of a furnace were a half-dozen flush coal scuttles. The furnace door creaked as they opened it.

As Colm watched the warehouse's entrance, Brueghel loaded the charcoal into the furnace, sprayed it with lighter fluid and lit it with a match. After it worked into a steady blaze, they loaded in the woman's body and packed it with more coal. They shut the door and waited.

Once it had scorched up past recognition, Brueghel left.

Colm lingered, lit a cigarette and then walked back to his apartment.

His clothes reeked of the smolder. He threw them in the rubbish bin. He made his mind up to kill Brueghel. Colm got him a month later as he was returning to his apartment building after dark. In a burlap mask, wielding a Thompson submachine gun, he sprayed Brueghel's insides against the black brick wall. He blamed some bootleggers Brueghel had done in the previous year. Confidential tip, warehouse raid, the weapon found stashed beneath the floorboards. He almost forgot the smell of her skin burning.

PART XXI

Leola Auden had figured out what happened to Brueghel. Colm knew that as he walked to the cafe to meet her. It was two rows of square, white-clothed tables across a vacancy of checkerboard floor that led to a polished, dark green counter. That afternoon, she was wearing a black dress with a matching cloche and gloves, daintily sipping from a blue cup. Colm had on a grey three-piece under his dark blue trench coat, and a pair of brown oxfords he had just polished.

"We've only spoken twice in the last year," said Colm as he sat down in front of her with his drink, coffee he had spiked with gin.

"We've had no reason," she said, lighting a cigarette. "You see, I've blundered into an odd situation. As part of another investigation, I've gained possession of a cache of ancient Mesopotamian musical instruments. But I've been unable to sell it through my museum contacts. The government would seize it from any legitimate buyers. I'm looking into private collectors."

"Are you asking if I know of any?"

Leola dragged her cigarette.

"I'd have to take at look at what you have first."

"Then let's take a look."

He took his time walking to the docks from his apartment that evening. The light snowfall reminded him of the day he left Brymner after the strike. The same dull emptiness gutted his stomach as he trudged to the row of beige shipping containers along the lip of the dark water. After he found the right one, he stopped and lit a cigarette, then stared at a passing vessel pumping fumes into the starry sky. He dragged the cherry to the filter and stubbed it out with his shoe.

When he opened the container, Leola was standing there in the hollow cavity, aiming an FN Model 1910 pistol at him.

"Personal or professional?" Colm asked her.

"I was close with Brueghel," she said. "Before he became what he was. I owe this to him. And to be quite honest, I've never been that fond of you."

Leola pulled the trigger. The darkness flared yellow.

Colm heard the gunshot, felt the sting in his guts, and knew it was over.

He stepped outside and dropped to his knees. Then he watched the blood from his torso form a wretched angel in the drifting dust. It was his only sacred utterance in forty years, and one he feared was not enough to save him from the hellfire he'd spent a lifetime earning.

ABOUT THE AUTHOR

Nicholas Wagner is a writer and independent filmmaker from Virginia. His previous stories include the novellas *Tout, Curse of the Jesuit, Her Soft Hours* and *A Ruin of Mercies*, the independent films *Shelter for the Bloodstained Soul* and *The Holy Sound*, as well as the comic book *Bring Me the Butcher's Knife*.

Made in the USA
Middletown, DE
16 September 2024